Praise for the writing of Sedonia Guillone

The Completeness of Celia Flynn

"The name **Sedonia Guillone** on an ebook has become a prime indicator of great stories and scorching, out-of-the-ordinary, sensuality. *The Completeness of Celia Flynn* is no exception to this rule."

– Annie, *Euro Reviews*

"Ms. Guillone spins us a haunting tale of innocent love, trembling desires, regret of lost time, and rediscovering the true joys of life."

– Jasmina Vallombrosa, *TCM Reviews*

The Satisfaction of Celia Flynn

"The night that [Celia's] men created for her will have you not only panting with desire, but envious of the relationship and emotional connection these people have between them."

– *Two Lips Reviews*

"The heat between the four lovers is only is only out done by the obvious affection they feel for each other. Four Angels."

– Lynn, *Fallen Angels*

LooseId®

ISBN 10: 1-59632-520-8
ISBN 13: 978-1-59632-520-3
THE COMPLETENESS OF CELIA FLYNN
Copyright © 2006 by Sedonia Guillone
Originally released in e-book format in October 2006

Cover Art by April Martinez

Printed in the U.S.A. by
Lightning Source, Inc.
1246 Heil Quaker Blvd
La Vergne TN 37086
www.lightningsource.com

THE COMPLETENESS OF CELIA FLYNN

With bonus story

The Satisfaction of Celia Flynn

Sedonia Guillone

Chapter One

Ballykillmarrick, Ireland, 1913

As she'd done a thousand times in the past seven years, Celia lay back on the straw, enjoying the feel of Robert's dark head resting on her stomach. She watched him leisurely twiddling a piece of straw between his teeth. Freddie and Patrick were on either side of her, their heads close to hers.

Yet somehow, this time, something was...different. Her heart pumped harder than usual and her blood ran like liquid fire through her veins.

There seemed no better way to spend her nineteenth birthday than here in the abandoned barn of Robert's family's farm, staring up at the rafters, surrounded by her three best childhood friends.

Except that something was happening to her. The sensation of it was like falling. Only she was lying on her back.

She reached out and touched Robert's dark hair. It was so soft under her fingertips.

"Mmm, Ceil, ye've an angel's touch," Robert murmured.

Celia's breath caught softly. The feel of his hair under her fingertips resonated deep inside her, stirring deep vibrations between her thighs. She lifted her hand from Robert's head as if he were on fire.

He seemed not to notice.

She glanced to either side of her. Patrick held his notebook, deep in the act of composing a new poem. All his poems were about her, she realized with a blinding flash. So blind she'd been all this time. His sandy brown hair invited her touch as well. She resisted.

And Freddie, to her other side, had just a few days ago described to her his ideal woman. She hadn't registered what he was saying then, but the description of a slim willowy girl with pale freckled skin and waves of dark long hair had fit her to perfection.

None of the three lads, now in their twentieth years, seemed to be on the search for girlfriends, always content to be with her. Nor was she looking, either. She was never happier than she was with her three friends.

Friends! What were they then that they caused her to feel this way? These sensations ripped through her body, making her want each one of them in her arms, inside her, their lips against hers?

She felt suddenly surrounded, not by her playmates, but by grown men. The pulsing between her legs rose to a pitch and her breasts tingled, her nipples tightening. She suddenly wanted Robert to hold her and kiss her, to explore her with his hands and mouth. In fact, she wanted the same from Patrick and Freddie.

Fear gripped her in that moment. Her skin prickled with its icy touch and her heart set to rioting in her chest as she realized the truth. She loved all three men. They were her life.

Terrified, Celia wondered if Freddie or Patrick or Robert had noticed her crash into womanhood. Her breasts rose and fell heavily with her ragged breathing, and she sought desperately to recapture childhood.

Suddenly, the fact that she'd been waiting for them to wish her happy birthday went from being an annoyance to a lifesaving topic of conversation.

"All three of you forgot my birthday, it seems," she said in a tight voice.

Robert sat up, looking at her sheepishly. "Oh, Celia. I'm so sorry! Was it today? I'll make it up to you, I swear."

Freddie sat up now also. "I'm sorry, too, Ceil." He was equally as sheepish.

Celia sat up and looked at Patrick, who had now risen up on his elbows. He regarded her shamefacedly. "You should have given us warning. We would have been prepared."

Celia swatted his arm. "I can't believe you!" Her cheeks burned with her indignation. "I've never forgotten any of your birthdays! In ten years of friendship, not once. And this is what it comes to, then, eh?" She looked again at Robert, whose sheepish smile had turned to mischief. A funny tickly feeling fluttered in her stomach. She looked from one man to the next, seeing they all wore the same mischievous look now. A tiny smile teased the corners of her lips. "What's going on, then?"

Robert's dark eyes flickered in the others' directions just before the three of them burst into raucous laughter. They jostled Celia gently around, tickling and tumbling her until her hair was mussed and her face flushed bright pink. Finally, when she was nearly breathless, they stopped and let her up.

"We had you going there for a bit, didn't we?" Patrick said, laughing.

"Come now, Ceil," Freddie said. "You really think we'd forget?"

Celia, feeling sheepish herself, smiled as she picked bits of straw out of her messy hair. "I'm sorry. I should have had more faith. But we'd been here forever, and no one said a word!"

Robert grinned and poked at her ribs. "It wouldn'a worked so well, now, would it, if we had?"

Celia crossed her arms protectively over her ribs as she laughed. "No, I suppose not."

Robert reached into the pocket of his trousers and pulled out a small box, which he handed to her. "The three of us chipped in for this. Freddie got it in Dublin."

Celia fingered the small red velvet box, the kind that came from a jeweler. "What's this?" she asked in a whisper as her heart began to jump.

"Go on, Ceil," Freddie urged. "Open it."

Gingerly, Celia lifted the lid, catching her breath when she saw what was inside. A delicate gold chain with a heart pendant nestled in the satiny folds of the box. "I can't believe it!" She stared at the lovely charm, her heart feeling fuzzy and sweet in her chest. "It's so beautiful!" She looked up, her gaze passing to each man's face. They were watching her expectantly.

"Do you really like it?" Robert asked.

"I love it! Thank you!"

"Put it on, then," Patrick said.

Celia smiled. "All right." Delicately she lifted the necklace from the box. Robert reached out and offered to help her. She lifted her hair up while he fastened it at the nape of her neck, his fingertips brushing her skin as he did so. Celia shivered lightly at his touch.

She let her hair down and touched her fingertips to the gold heart now resting against her dress, just under the hollow of her throat. She smiled at them. "Thank you all so much," she said. "This is the most beautiful present I've ever gotten."

"I'm glad, Ceil." Freddie leaned over and embraced her.

In Freddie's arms, Celia felt the change again, that acute awareness of her three masculine companions. Freddie felt warm and strong in her arms and a strange, languid weakness came over her.

Gently, she pulled away and embraced Patrick. Patrick was an athlete as well as a poet and she could feel the sinew of his back muscles under her hands. The heat from his body came through his shirt and before they parted, she caught a whiff of his earthy scent.

Robert was the strongest. His father was a farmer and Robert had grown up helping him plow the fields of potatoes they grew. Robert's chest and back were broad and strong from heavy work. Celia felt the stirring between her legs again as she had when she was caressing his hair earlier. "Happy birthday, Celia," Robert said close to her ear.

Robert's breath was warm on her skin, and when Celia slowly pulled away, she was breathing more heavily. She could feel Freddie and Patrick's eyes on her and she felt surrounded by their masculine strength and heat. She began to tremble. "What's the matter, Ceil?" Robert said. "Are you cold?"

Celia shook her head as she stared at him, captured by the dusky velvet of his dark eyes. "No," she whispered.

Robert reached up and touched her cheek. "Your skin is so soft."

"Th-thank you," Celia stammered. Her stomach lurched wildly and the palms of her hands began to feel moist. How was it that her childhood friends whom she had known her whole life suddenly seemed complete strangers?

She felt a hand on her hair, stroking it gently. Glancing 'round, she saw it was Patrick. He moved closer to her and lifted the fall of her hair to his face, breathing in the scent of her dark waves.

Then her hand was in Freddie's and he was tracing the skin on her knuckles with his fingertips. Her breathing grew heavier and her eyes fluttered closed. Instinctively, she tilted her head back just before she felt Robert's lips on hers. He pressed down gently at first, then harder, bidding her lips to part with his tongue. No one had ever kissed her before, and she felt a jolt of heat when Robert's tongue touched hers, tentatively at first, then languorously tasting the inside of her lips.

Patrick was still stroking her hair and pressing it to his face, and Freddie, who still held her hand, had put his other hand on her thigh, stroking it down to her knee and back up again, reaching a little farther up her skirt with each stroke.

Celia moaned, overwhelmed with the pleasure of being kissed and touched. Robert's hand had been on Celia's cheek, his thumb brushing the soft, lightly freckled skin, but as his kisses deepened, he trailed his fingers downward from her cheek to her throat and chest to close softly around her right breast. Tenderly, he squeezed it, lightly rubbing her nipple through her blouse.

Celia moaned softly. She felt herself falling backward, not knowing whether it was purely from her surrender or the pressure of their hands on various parts of her body bidding her to lie back.

Freddie's hands were roaming over both her thighs, over her stockings and upward, his fingers brushing the bare skin underneath her garters. The supple skin of her inner thighs tingled under his touch, sending jolts of heat between her legs, causing her woman's musk to gather and seep out.

Celia's skirt had ridden up, gathering around her waist, and Freddie's fingers were venturing closer and closer to the moist heat of her sex. Tentatively, with sweet gentleness, he brushed his fingertips over her underpants where the thin material covered her slit and her moisture had begun to saturate the cloth.

Celia moaned with the utter intensity of the pleasure they gave her. Robert and Patrick were taking turns kissing her, each with a hand on one of her breasts, while Freddie continued to run his fingertips lightly along her slit.

Perhaps it was then that the fight began inside of her, stirred by the fear she had felt earlier when she knew she loved all three of them. Her mother had never approved of her friendship with the three lads, always telling her they would lead her into sin. Celia loved her mother and wanted to honor her, but she could never bear the thought of staying away from her friends. She craved their company and the light they brought into her life, especially after she lost her father. Then her older brothers began courting girls, leaving them with little time for their baby sister. Over the years, Robert, Freddie, and Patrick had seen her through great suffering, and she loved them. And as long as they had been only like brothers, Celia had been able to ignore her mother's warnings about sin.

But in that moment, with her body's surrender to untold erotic pleasure, Celia heard her mother's voice of warning come crashing in, not realizing how strong Margaret Flynn's influence had become. Celia felt suddenly evil and dirty. Giving her body to one man outside of marriage was sinful enough. But to three? And all at once?

Celia's eyes flew open and she had cried out for them to stop, sitting up in the straw, pushing her skirt down. She covered her face with her hands, crying, surrounded by her three bewildered, would-be lovers.

"What is it, Celia?" Robert asked. "Were we hurting you?"

Celia shook her head, refusing to look at them.

"Then what?" She heard Patrick ask. Glancing up, she saw him look at Freddie and Robert questioningly, but they could only look back at him, their facial expressions equally as confused. She put her face in her hands again.

"It's wrong!" Celia cried. "We were friends!" She continued sobbing.

Robert reached out and touched Celia's arm. "It's all right, Celia. We love you."

"Please look at us, Celia," Freddie pleaded.

But Celia felt hysteria sweep over her. "I can't!" she cried. Then, propelled by her guilt and self-loathing, she jumped up and ran out, not stopping until she was back in the village, in her house, locked in her room.

She remained there, curled in the fetal position on her bed as the room darkened. Her mum knocked on the door to ask her help preparing supper, but Celia begged off, claiming a horrible headache.

A little bit after that, her brother Liam knocked on the door and poked his head in. "Your lads are here to see ye, Ceil."

Icy fear ripped through her body, prickling down her arms and legs. She sat up. "Tell them I'm ill. I can't come down."

Liam's dark eyebrows drew together. "Did they do something to hurt ye?"

"Of course not. You're so suspicious. Da wouldn'a asked such a question." She was clear they'd done nothing wrong. She was the sinner here.

"Our da was a dreamer." Liam sighed. "God rest his soul. You want me to tell them you're sick?"

She nodded. "Aye. I can't come down."

"All right."

Celia lay back on the bed, fresh tears streaming from eyes she'd thought had gone dry in the last few hours. Oh, God, but she loved those lads! How could this have happened? It was unnatural. Her mum always told her that about her friendship with Robert, Patrick and Freddie. Margaret Flynn was right.

Celia sighed heavily and turned onto her side, wishing she could go to sleep and never wake up, especially since now she knew she could never see those three young men again.

Chapter Two

Three years later...

Sinner or not, Celia wanted her lads back. She stared out the window, fingering the gold heart on the delicate chain they'd given her before she'd so horribly pushed them away. She'd never removed it, even during the year before they'd gone down into the trenches, even while she'd been going with Donal.

Celia tortured herself with memories of that horrible day in which she'd pushed the men she loved from her life. After they'd come to see her the evening she refused to come down, she'd seen them only once, and she'd fought them, pushing until they were forced to turn away and go back to their homes, leaving Celia's life with a black hole that had once been filled with love and sweetness. It was shortly after that that Celia took up with Donal, intending to marry him and live a conventional life that would not arouse anyone's ire, especially her mother's. But then the war had broken out and all the young men were gone.

Celia had given Donal her virginity in the backseat of his father's motorcar two days before Donal left. But even before that, they had spent many hours together, stealing deep, sensuous kisses, exploring each other's body with their hands and mouths. Donal had loved to go down on Celia, and had spent much time pleasuring her, caressing her sweet spot with his tongue until her back arched with the release of her climax. Her memories of the erotic pleasure they had given each other had carried her through his absence, and though she had not been madly in love with him, she had waited faithfully for his return. But Donal wasn't going to return. The Gerrys had seen to that.

Celia's hand went to the necklace she wore, her gold heart on its delicate chain. Gingerly she fingered the smooth charm, remembering the lads who had given it her. Freddie, Patrick and Robert also had gone for soldiers, all three. It was they whom Celia loved and missed the most, even when she wouldn't admit it to herself. She had spent the last two years knitting them socks, which she sent in care packages, with tins of chocolates, when she could get them, along with letters of profuse apologies for what she'd done to them, pleas for forgiveness, and declarations of love.

Celia always regretted what she did and never stopped missing her three men. Donal, though handsome and considerate, hadn't had the same mysterious and deep connection to her heart as Robert, Freddie and Patrick. She learned from great heartache how special they were and what a horrible mistake she'd made.

As far as she knew, all three were still alive, but she didn't know where they were or what had happened to them. Now, however, she clung to the hope they'd be coming back.

In the summer of 1917, the government commissioned the Flynn home, which was the largest in Ballykillmarrick, to be used as a temporary, makeshift hospital for returning soldiers whose wounds were minor. There were bedrooms to spare, for Tom Flynn, Celia's father, had died nine years before when Celia was only twelve, and her two older brothers, Sean and Liam, had been killed in the trenches. The government offered Celia and her mother a small income for the use of their home and for their help. They had agreed, and in a matter of days, the Flynn home had been transformed into a war hospital of sorts to aid soldiers with their transition to normal life.

Celia moved into her mother's room so that hers could house the nurse from the Voluntary Aid Detachment, while Sean and Liam's old rooms could accommodate the patients. Extra cots were placed in each room, and Celia changed the linens, opened the windows to let in fresh air, and put flowers in vases on the bedside tables to bring some softness and cheer to the men who would be staying there.

The night before the soldiers were to arrive, Celia lay wide awake, her mind alive with hopeful fantasies of living in a house full of the men she'd loved. She prayed that if they came back, they'd forgive her and give her another chance. The prospect made Celia's body fill with heat, a warm, pulsing fire that ignited in the secret fold between her legs and spread through her body, filling her breasts, making her nipples tingle and ache to be touched. She hadn't been with a man since Donal had left for the front with all the others. And after all that time, the mere thought of a male presence, that masculine energy and strength close to her made her breathing grow heavier and her heartbeat quicken.

For the first time since her father died, Celia began to pray again. She had been angry with God for taking her father, and had refused to pray after that. But the three years of intense loneliness and suffering had wrought a change in her. God had not told her to push the lads out of her life. It was He who had given them to her in the first place.

No. She had come to understand that her own fears and her mother's angry voice inside her had caused her actions, not God's love. Every night before bed, she dropped to her knees, praying for their safe return. She gave God her vow that if they did come back and still loved her, she would not break their hearts the way she had three years ago.

She often thought back to that day in the barn, cringing with shame and pain when she reached the part of the memory where she'd run away.

But tonight, with her blood pulsing and her body aroused, Celia dared to imagine what might have happened had she allowed herself to surrender completely. Perhaps Freddie would have undone her garters so he could slip off her panties and caress her bare slit with his fingertips. Perhaps he would have rubbed and teased the slick pinkness of her swollen clit, sliding his fingers in and out of her opening while she moaned.

Perhaps Patrick or Robert might have unbuttoned her blouse, taking down the straps of her brassiere so they could fondle and suckle her bare breasts. Then, one by one, they'd open their trousers and mount her, nesting their hardness deep between her legs. They would have been gentle as they took her virginity, sliding slowly and carefully in and out. She probably would already have had an orgasm from having her breasts and her sex pleasured at the same time with three pairs of hands and three mouths. But Celia knew she would have enjoyed feeling them inside of her, having their pleasure too, feeling their bodies tremble when they came, feeling the warm pulsing of their seed spilling into her womb...

Celia rose from her mother's bed, unable to lie still any longer. She put her wrap on over her nightgown and went into the living room. In the quiet darkness, she lay down on the sofa and spread her legs, letting her wrap fall open. Celia pulled her nightgown up to her waist and put her hand to her slit, catching her breath softly when her fingertips first touched the swollen pink lips. Celia slid her fingers further in and began rubbing lightly over the moist nubbin of flesh. She closed her eyes, biting down on her lip to stifle her moans of pleasure. She rubbed and kneaded the slick flesh until a climax began to build, mounting stronger each time she pictured Robert or Freddie or Patrick inside of her, each one at his turn, thrusting feverishly while the others watched, delighting in the sight of her naked body, the sounds of her moans and the sweaty scent of her musk pervading the air...

Celia arched her pelvis upward as the spasms of pleasure began their release. She kept up the light fast rubbing on her clit until the last tremor passed and she lay limp against the cushions. She pushed her nightgown back down and covered herself with her wrap, then relaxed, staring into the shadows.

Soon, she was too sleepy to get up and go back into her mother's room. Celia pulled a small crocheted afghan from the back of the sofa and spread it over herself. Her mind and body were quieter after her release, but her heart still ached for her lads. If they were here with her now, she would have curled up with them, kissing and stroking them before falling asleep.

Celia closed her eyes and prayed. "Please, God," she whispered, her eyelids growing heavy. "Let it be Your will that they come home to me safe and alive, all three of them. Let them be restored to me. Please…"

* * *

"Celia!"

Celia blinked her eyes when she heard her name. The tone was harsh, jolting her from sleep. Celia looked up at her mother's pinched face. Mum's brown eyes held a reproachful glare, and the lines around her frowning lips creased angrily. She wore an apron over her blouse and skirt, showing she'd already begun her day in the kitchen.

Celia felt immediately guilty and sat up, holding the afghan to her front. "I'm sorry, Mum." She reached up to rub the sleep from her eyes with the heel of her hand. "I couldn't sleep. I missed my room."

Mum's face softened a bit. "We've a lot to do before they come. Get dressed now." She turned and left the room.

Hearing her mother go back into the kitchen, Celia rose slowly from the sofa and folded the afghan. She thought of her father as she set the little pink and green blanket back in its place, remembering how she used to curl up in it next to him while he read. She had always run to him when her mother was harsh with her, letting him stroke her hair and soothe her. "It's not your fault, Ceil," he always said. "Your mum, she's bitter. She gave up her dream of being an artist to marry me and have you and the lads." He always sounded terribly sad when he told her that, and Celia had once asked him if he'd ever tried to encourage her to pursue her art. Da nodded, a mournful expression on his face. "I did try," he answered. "I told her many times, 'Go to Dublin, Maggie, and study. Go to France, even, if you wish. I'll pay your way.' But she wouldn't."

Celia started for her mother's room to dress.

"There's a pot of tea in the kitchen!" she heard her mother call out from the kitchen.

Celia sighed. That was her mother's way of saying good morning in a nicer way than she had moments before.

"Thanks!" Celia called back before going in and closing the door.

* * *

At half past ten, a motorcar pulled up in front of the house. Celia heard it and hastily checked her appearance in the hall mirror, patting her large bun into place and pinching some color into her clear, pale cheeks. Then she joined her mother on the front stoop.

The driver's door opened and a man in army dress got out as the back doors opened. Two young men in officers' uniforms and a VAD in her nun-like uniform emerged. Celia didn't recognize the first lad as she watched him sling his pack over his shoulder and start toward the house. She studied him to see what was wrong, but he seemed fine. The other officer's back was to her. He was having more difficulty and leaned heavily on a cane as he pulled his pack off the seat.

Celia knew who it was. Though she hadn't yet seen his face, Celia's heart quickened when she saw his dark hair and broad shoulders. He put his weight on the cane as he slung on his pack, refusing the driver's offer of help just before turning around.

When he did, Celia let out a small cry and flew down the front walk. Hot tears came to her eyes, but she fought them back as she approached. As they drew closer, Celia felt a jolt of emotional pain in her heart at how Robert limped, and how haunted his once-mischievous dark eyes now looked.

Robert came to a stop in front of Celia, and they stared at each other. "Robert!" Celia whispered, unable to restrain a joyful smile. The tears she had fought a moment before now gathered with such force of her emotions that she could no longer hold them back.

She covered her face with her hands and sobbed.

"Celia," she heard him say gently. She felt his familiar touch on her arm. Celia uncovered her face and looked at him. His eyes were sad, but he smiled at her and took her hand.

"I suppose that introductions aren't necessary," the man who'd been driving the motorcar said cheerfully. He spoke with an English accent.

Robert looked him. "We're...old friends, Lieutenant Graves."

At this, Celia cried some more at the sound of forgiveness in his voice. "We grew up together," she added.

Mum, who'd been hovering in the background, now stepped forward. "Why don't we all go in? We can have some tea and get acquainted. I expect Robert's family will be here any moment as well."

No sooner had she spoken the words than another motorcar pulled up in front of the house. Robert's parents and two sisters got out of the car. His other two brothers were still in France.

Between the family reunion and helping her mother prepare meals for the household, Celia had no time that day to speak privately with Robert. She divided her time between seeing to him and the other lad, whose name was Kenneth Neary. Kenneth's damages of war, though not physical, became obvious to Celia within the first hour. The young man sat quietly alone on a lawn chair in the backyard, speaking to no one, smoking one cigarette after the other. When Celia went outside to offer him tea, he jumped up at her approach, his eyes looking wildly about him. The VAD, a kindly woman about her mother's age, told Celia that Mr. Neary had shell shock, a condition that could be serious enough to have a man discharged from service. Kenneth, she explained, had spent time in a special hospital in Edinburgh, Scotland that treated officers with his condition. He wasn't stable enough to go back down to the front and the military had discharged him.

Celia tried to engage Kenneth in friendly conversation, but to no avail. The lad could only answer her in short sentences before his mouth began to twitch so horribly he couldn't speak.

Finally, in the evening before bed, after Robert's family had left and the supper things were cleaned and put away, Celia went to Liam's old room where Robert was staying. Robert was there, sitting in a chair by the window, staring out. In his hand he held an unlit cigarette. "Robert?"

He turned around. He smiled when their eyes met and put out his cane to stand up.

Celia came over and stood in front of him, her stomach jumping wildly around inside. "You can sit."

But Robert shook his head and moved away from the chair, leaning on the windowsill. "You sit down, Ceil," he told her. "I've done enough sitting these days. And you've been working all day to take care of us." He gestured to the chair. "Go ahead."

Celia reluctantly sat, looking up at Robert. "Are you settled in all right?"

Robert gazed at her, twiddling the unlit cigarette around in his fingers. "Aye, I'm fine." He looked down at the cigarette. "I wasn't sure if I should light it."

Celia looked at him. Robert had never smoked a cigarette in his life before now. "Go ahead," she answered. "Liam smoked in here all the time." She reached out and handed him a bowl from the table beside the chair. Her mother had wiped the bowl clean, but Liam had always used it for his ashes. Celia watched Robert pull a book of matches from his pocket and strike one, cupping his hands over the cigarette as he lit it. He opened the window and blew the smoke outside into the summer air.

"Robert."

He turned to look at her, softness coming into his dark eyes. "I know what you're going to say, Ceil," he told her gently. "You don't have to." He took a deep drag on the cigarette and blew the smoke outside before turning back to her. "We were babes then. Another lifetime. I see things differently now."

Celia nodded as her eyes filled with tears. She thought of her prayer the night before. It seemed God had answered it. "So do I," she whispered. She reached up and wiped at her tears, then stood up and went to Robert. "Robert? Do you still…" She trailed off and looked down, afraid of what he might answer.

"Love you?"

Celia glanced at him and looked down again, embarrassed and afraid. "Aye."

Robert mashed his cigarette into the bowl and set it down on the windowsill. He reached out and touched Celia's cheek. "I do. I never stopped. Neither have Patrick and Freddie." He brushed his thumb lightly across her skin. "We've missed you something fierce."

Celia began to cry harder and Robert pulled her to him, caressing her hair. She wrapped her arms around him. Through the smell of cigarettes, he still had the same earthy scent she had loved. "I'm so sorry!" she cried into his shirt.

But Robert stroked her hair. "Shhh. It's going to be all right. I'm back. God willing, we'll all be together again."

Celia lifted her head and looked up at him. He leaned down and kissed her, gently slipping his tongue between her lips. Celia forgot her tears as she surrendered to the deep kiss.

Robert danced his tongue against hers, tasting her and loving her with his gentle kiss for several moments before lifting his face away to look at her again. He smiled. "You've stopped your crying."

Celia smiled back and wiped at her eyes. "I'm being selfish. After what you've been through, and here I am crying on your shoulder."

"I don't mind." Robert leaned on his cane and reached out his hand to smooth back Celia's hair. "Before you go thinking how awful you are, let me tell you something. Those trenches are hell on Earth. You can't imagine it, Ceil. You see your mates get blown up in your face and the like. Day after day in the mud with rats and death, you begin to think that's all there is, and you don't want to live anymore. But today, when we pulled up in front of your house and I saw you standing there, looking at me so happy, I felt hope for the first time."

Celia took Robert's hand and held it to her cheek. "I've missed you so. I never want to be separated from you again. Not for a minute." She pressed her lips into the palm of his hand and closed her eyes. She heard Robert's breathing grow a bit ragged.

"Will you come to me tonight?" he whispered.

Celia opened her eyes and looked at him. Her pulse quickened. "Aye, Robert, I will. After my mum falls asleep."

Robert looked down and Celia felt him tense. "You're afraid of her."

Celia sighed. "I don't want her to try and stop me."

Robert squeezed Celia's hand. "You're a grown woman now. You've got to have your own life."

Celia nodded. "I know. I feel guilty."

"For what?"

"For having my heart's desire when she didn't have hers."

"And what was her heart's desire?" Robert asked.

"She wanted to be an artist."

"So what happened?"

"She didn't study because she had her family. My da tried to get her to go, but she wouldn't."

Robert brought Celia's hand to his lips and kissed it, causing a warm thrill up her arm. "That's not your fault, Ceil."

Celia closed her eyes, enjoying the warm tremors of arousal pulsing in her body. "You're right, Robert," she whispered. "The last two and a half years have been a hard teacher."

Robert kissed Celia's hand again. "I'm glad I'm here," he said softly.

Celia smiled at him. "Me, too."

Robert released her hand. "Go on, then. I'll see you in a bit."

Celia paused and gazed at him one moment before she left to take her bath and help her mother prepare the house for the next day.

Chapter Three

Celia lay awake, waiting for her mother to fall asleep so she could go to Robert. She wished she could just have told her mother her intention, but, to her own shame, she had cowered from the task. Had it been Da, Celia knew she would just have said to him, 'Da, I want to be with Robert tonight.' For even if her father were to disapprove, she wouldn't have felt threatened with losing his love. Mum was a different matter, and Celia had not yet shored up her courage.

Her mother's breathing eventually grew steady and deep, and Celia knew she was sleeping. She was just about to rise from the bed when a bloodcurdling scream tore through the house. Celia and her mother both sat bolt upright.

"What in God's name?" Mum looked at Celia, her eyes wide with fear.

Celia's heart lurched in her chest and she jumped from the bed. "I'll go see. Perhaps one of them is in pain."

"Celia! That's what the nurse is for!"

"I know that, Mum," Celia pulled her wrap on and went to the door. "But I want to make sure Robert's all right. He's been through hell, you know!"

Celia went out of the bedroom and down the hall where light from under the door of Sean's old room shone in the darkness. Kenneth Neary was in that room, she could hear him crying and whimpering. She stopped outside the door and listened. The VAD was with him, speaking to him in soothing tones, and Celia realized he'd had a nightmare. She cracked open the door and poked her head in. The older woman was sitting on the edge of the bed, holding the young man's hands. She turned when she heard the door open. "Everything's all right," she assured Celia. "He's had a nightmare."

Celia looked at Kenneth's face, red and drawn, his eyes like those of a frightened animal's. "Does he need anything?" she asked. "A glass of warm milk, perhaps?"

The woman smiled. "No, thank you, dear. It's best if he gets back to sleep as soon as possible."

Celia nodded. "All right, then. Good night." She turned and closed the door behind her. Poor lad, she thought as she went further down the hall to Robert's room. He, too, had the light on, and when Celia opened the door, he was in bed, propped up against the pillows, smoking. The shirt of his pajama top was open, revealing his broad chest with its dusting of silky dark hair covering the muscles in a triangular pattern between his nipples. A trail of it funneled down the center of his hard stomach, disappearing under the waistband of his pajama pants.

Her body responded instantly to the sight, getting moist and melty between her thighs. She closed the door behind her and went to him.

Robert smiled as she approached. He mashed the cigarette out into the bowl and pulled aside the blanket, making room for her in the bed.

She stopped at the edge of the bed, looking down. "He had a nightmare, the poor lad."

Robert nodded. "I know exactly how he feels." Then he patted the mattress. "Come, Celia," he said softly.

She sat down and put her hand to Robert's cheek. "Do you need anything? Some water or tea?"

Robert reached up and brushed his thumb along her cheek and across her lips. "Only one thing." He slipped his hand around her head, entwining his fingers in her hair. Gently he pulled her down to kiss him, letting his other hand roam over her back.

She returned his kiss. His lips were warm and she breathed in the heady mixture of cigarettes and cologne that clung to his skin. Her eyes fluttered closed as heat radiated through her entire body. With one hand she reached up and squeezed his shoulder, reveling in the male strength that emanated from him. Slowly, she sank down on top of him, kicking off her slippers so she could stretch out on the bed next to him and press the length of her body against his. She felt as if she were sinking into the most delicious pool. God! How wonderful it was to feel a man in her arms again! The stark loneliness of her life until that day struck her as Robert's touch and kisses began to ease it away. Her hunger for love had been very deep.

She plunged her tongue against Robert's, moaning softly as she tasted him and she rolled onto her side, freeing her hand to explore his strong body. The sensitive skin of her fingertips drank in the hard slopes of muscle, the warm, masculine skin, and the soft dark hairs on his chest, the smooth skin of his small nipples, which, she noticed, tightened under her fingertips.

Robert's breathing grew heavier, his chest heaving under her hand. He reached up, tugging gently at her wrap to pull it back, over her bare shoulders, feeling for her breasts over the thin material of her nightgown.

She moaned when his hands closed over one, then the other, squeezing gently, kneading the tips. They pebbled into aroused stiffness, sending jolts of heat into her body. She slid her hand over Robert's stomach, her fingertips grazing the taut flesh just underneath the waistband of his pajamas. Robert heaved a ragged breath under her hand as she drew closer to his erection, and he gathered up her nightgown, drawing it upward. "Take this off, Ceil," he whispered.

She kissed him again. "All right," she whispered back. She sat up and reached to turn off the bedside lamp before undressing, but Robert grasped her arm.

"No, don't. Please leave it on." His dark eyes had grown dusky, the lids heavier. "You're so pretty. I want to see you."

Her cheeks flushed hot, but she wanted so much to please Robert, she withdrew her hand from the lamp and pulled her nightgown over her head, letting it drop to the floor.

Robert caught his breath and lay, watching her. He reached up and caressed the swell of her breast with his fingertips, brushing them over the cherry red nipple and rosy aureole, which tightened to a peak under his soft touch. "To me, you're the prettiest lass I've ever seen."

She closed her eyes, melting under his touch and his praise. "Thank you," she whispered as he trailed his fingertips between her breasts, down her soft woman's stomach, to the springy dark curls between her thighs.

He looked up at her as he smoothed his palm over her thigh, resting it there. "Celia, listen. I took shrapnel in my hip."

She put her hand gently over his. "I know."

"It will heal, mostly. But right now, I can't...get on top." He looked embarrassed and her heart wrung painfully for him.

"It's all right." She parted her thighs, bidding him to slip his hand between them. Her eyes fluttered closed at the brush of his fingertips on the sensitive skin of her inner thighs and moist slit. "Until then, we'll find other ways." She lay back down next to him and resumed her exploration of his body, at the same time seeking deep, hot kisses.

Robert caressed her breasts and hips, then reached down again between her thighs, sliding his fingertips between her labia, seeking the sensitive nub that caused her to moan when he found it and began rubbing.

Celia slid her hand over Robert's stomach, under the waistband of his pajama bottoms. He moaned when her fingers moved down the nest of dark hair to close lightly around his smooth hardness. She stroked his hard cock gently up and down, from head to base while she kissed him, loving the satiny feel of the skin over the tight muscle. She even dared to slip her hand lower, over the heavy sac of his balls, gently squeezing them, encouraged by his groans of pleasure.

His surrender to her heightened her blaze and she plunged her tongue deeply into his mouth, suckling it hungrily while she continued to stroke his cock, teasing the little opening at the tip with her index finger.

Robert slid two fingers into her, moving them in and out of the swollen pinkness. She moaned and opened her legs, desperate for his cock inside her. She started to pull down the pajamas, but Robert stayed her hand suddenly with his. "Wait, Ceil. Now you should turn the light off. I don't want you to see my scars."

She looked into Robert's eyes, seeing fear in them for the first time since she'd known him. She reached up and touched his cheek. "Let me see them, Robert," she coaxed gently. "I don't want you to feel ashamed." She caressed his cheek, kissing him softly on the lips until she felt the tension leave his body and he took his hand away.

Slowly, she lowered the pajamas, pulling them down past his hip and buttocks, stopping at his knees. Then she looked at his hip. The skin was, indeed, horribly damaged where the shrapnel had torn it. It was raw and puckered, and she understood why Robert had been worried. She leaned down and lightly kissed the angry-looking redness. Then she looked up at him and smiled.

He was looking back at her, dark eyes shining through their glaze of desire. "You're a gentle lass, Celia," he said softly.

She brushed her fingertips over the damaged skin. "I'm just grateful you're alive," Then she put her head back down and captured his erection in her mouth. Her eyes fluttered closed at the pleasure of the velvety skin and hard muscle against her tongue, and she suckled it, her eager tongue tracing the contours of the plump head, suckling a drop of seed that seeped out, while reaching up at the same time to caress his chest and stomach.

She felt Robert's fingers lace through her hair, following the movement of her bobbing head. The sound of his soft moans filled her ears as the musky flavor of his cock filled her other senses.

Finally, when more droplets of seed seeped from the tiny opening, Robert grasped her arms. "Come up here," he whispered, gently tugging her. "Climb onto me."

She obediently rose to her knees and lifted one leg over and straddled him. He guided his cock into her wet opening. She moaned, seared by the pleasure of being penetrated, and in one swift motion she slid down, impaling herself on him to the base.

Robert groaned with the pleasure of the impact, watching her through heavy-lidded eyes. A crooked smile played on his lips, a return of the mischievous old Robert. "Pretend you're on horseback, Celia. Ride like the wind."

She started to move, but then stopped, bewildered, for she didn't know how it worked with her on top. She and Donal had only gone all the way that one time, and Donal had been on top. "I don't know what to do," she whispered.

But Robert smiled and held her hips. "You only need ask. Like this," he guided her motions, back and forth. "Like riding." He chuckled at first, then moaned as she took to the rhythm. "How's that?" he asked as she began to move a bit faster.

Delicious heat shot through her sex, sparks of intense pleasure where his cock ground against her little nub. "It's wonderful." Her own voice was throaty and breathless. That first time with Donal had hurt. She had bled and felt sore for several days. Her initial enthusiasm for sex had waned and she had prepared herself for a lifetime of unenjoyable service, not knowing that the flesh heals and eventually feels pleasure.

But now, sitting astride Robert, grinding and bucking against his groin, she relished the delicious rubbing against her swollen clitoris and all the parts of her sex, spots she had not known could feel so good. Back and forth she moved, the base of Robert's shaft rubbing right on her sweet spot. When she looked down at Robert, he was watching her, a large grin of enjoyment spread on his face. She bent over him, kissing him deeply as she continued her blissful ride.

Robert reached up and squeezed her breasts gently together, and when she lifted her face from his, he leaned his head forward, capturing the pink tips in his mouth each time her body thrust forward. She moaned each time his warm wet tongue brushed her nipples. The sensations caused a surge of heightened sensitivity between her legs, as if an invisible chord connected that part of her body to her breasts.

Her open enjoyment seemed to encourage Robert, and he raised himself on his elbows, lost in the pleasure of tasting her breasts. She gently captured his head in the crook of her arm and held him to her, moaning at the intense concentration of pleasure in her body.

The next she knew, the spasms of climax erupted in her nub and rippled through her. She struggled not to cry out from ecstasy lest the other people in the house hear her. "Robert! Robert!" she cried in a whisper as she collapsed on him.

Robert lay back and put his arms around her, caressing the soft skin of her back and hips. "That's my girl, Celia," he whispered into her hair. He kissed her temple. "Now you're ours again, aren't you?"

She smoothed back his hair and kissed his forehead. "Aye, Robert," she whispered between heavy breaths. "Aye. For always."

Robert smiled and closed his eyes, still kneading and caressing her hips and buttocks. "When you've caught your breath, Ceil, will you finish me off? It won't take long."

"Of course I will," she whispered. She began covering Robert's forehead and cheeks with small, soft kisses.

Robert moaned softly when she stirred her hips. "My sweet lass."

She rose up and began to ride him again, slowly at first, then faster, in hard strokes, tightening her sheath around Robert's still-hard cock. "Like this?"

"Aye, Ceil," Robert ground out. "Don't stop. I'm almost there."

She squeezed and stroked Robert's shaft with her body, all the while looking into his face, watching his features twitch and contort with his mounting climax. After a few moments, he let out a soft groan, his head rising and falling against the pillow in rhythms with the spasms of release. She felt the pulsing of his warm seed inside of her and gently collapsed on him again, spent from the exertion of her glorious ride.

The small bedroom filled with the sounds of their heavy breaths, and Robert closed his arms around her, nestling his face into her hair and neck. Bit by bit, their breathing steadied and they rested, languid and content. After a few moments, she rolled off of Robert and lay, stretched out alongside him, her eyes closed, her lips pressed to his shoulder.

"Celia, will you stay with me the night? I want to hold you."

Her body tensed. She hadn't thought past the first moments. It had never occurred to her to stay anywhere except in her mother's room. A pang of guilt shot through her chest at the thought of her mother in her bed, waiting, expecting Celia to come back, thinking what a harlot her daughter really was. She thought perhaps that staying in Mum's silent, condemning presence would be her penance for the sweetness and pleasure she'd dared to have.

"Celia? Is something wrong?"

Robert's voice pulled her from her guilty musings. She stroked his hair, now feeling guilty toward him. Robert needed her love and comfort. He'd completely forgiven her transgression against him and the others. His need was more important than her misplaced guilt. And besides, she wanted to stay with him more than anything. "Nothing's wrong, Robert. I love you."

Robert kissed her and pulled her more tightly against him. He lay on his uninjured side, molding her body to his like a pair of nesting spoons. "Do you still love Patrick and Freddie?"

"Aye," she said softly, "I do. Is that bad?"

Robert caressed her hair. "No, of course not. I don't get jealous with them. Maybe it's too strange, but we're part of each other. I don't worry." He paused and sighed. "When you went with Donal, I was insanely jealous. I couldn't bear the sight of you walking together. I can't explain the difference."

"I'm sorry, Robert." She cringed inwardly each time she thought of how she'd hurt him and the others.

"I already forgave you, Ceil. Long ago. I just pray you don't leave again. I love you as I always have. But now, I need you in a way I didn't."

His confession brought fresh tears to her eyes. She lifted Robert's hand to her lips and kissed it, thinking of a day long ago, on Murphy's Hill near Robert's farm. She had been twelve and the lads thirteen. They were playing at knights, and she, of course, had been the damsel in distress they were sworn to protect. As they made their oath, Robert had taken out his pocketknife and drawn blood from his hand. He bid Patrick and Freddie to do the same. They did, and the three boys mingled their blood, swearing their oath as blood brothers. What had begun as a game had taken a mysterious turn, and their simple action had bound them for real, weaving together their souls into one soul. She had felt it happen as she watched, even then, sensing a force rising up around them, something deep and strong. Something beyond words.

She felt that force now in Robert's arms, the strength of the love that had sealed itself into their hearts that day. And she prayed for the strength to honor it when she was tested. And tested she would be, if Margaret Flynn had anything to say. Which she would.

Chapter Four

Celia woke at dawn just as the first gray light came through the lace curtains. Robert's arms were still around her, and she longed to close her eyes and rest there. But her mother would need her help preparing breakfast and tidying the house, so she stirred gently, trying to get out of the bed without waking Robert.

Her attempt was unsuccessful and Robert opened his eyes, pulling her closer against him. "Do you have to go?" he murmured.

She turned and kissed his forehead. "Aye, Robert. I've a lot to do."

Robert sighed and released her. "I love you, Ceil." He watched her tenderly as she pulled on her nightgown and wrap.

Feeling so appreciated and warmed, she smiled. "I love you, too." How sweet it was to hear such words first thing upon rising! She leaned over and kissed Robert again before leaving.

Mum was already in the kitchen, frying onions in butter when Celia came down. The older woman's back was to her and Celia felt a wave of guilt wash through her when she didn't turn around.

"Good morning, Mum." She walked slowly to the kitchen table, where a loaf of bread sat ready for slicing. She picked up the bread knife and began to cut thick slices.

Her mother turned. "Good morning, Celia," she answered over the hissing and sputtering in her frying pan.

Celia searched her mother's face for the woman's feelings, but her expression was inscrutable. She set down the knife and took a few steps closer. "Are you mad at me?"

Mum sighed. "Mad is not the word I'd use."

Celia looked down, knowing the right word was probably more like horrified, or disgusted, or worse, ashamed. She went back to the table and picked up the knife to finish slicing the bread, all the while wishing her mother would turn back and smile at her or tell her, 'Come here, love,' and embrace her. But she didn't.

When the loaf was all sliced, Celia took it out to the dining room table, which she finished setting for breakfast. Now, there were as many places to set as when her father and brothers were alive and she was glad for the company. She liked having the lads and the VAD here. The nurse's name was Sarah, and she was very kind. She couldn't help comparing Sarah's gentle way to her mum's hardness. How she wished her mother would be kind as well and love her as she was!

When Celia went back into the kitchen for the butter, her mother was still at the stove, now frying sausages. Celia approached her and put her hand on her mother's shoulder, watching her face from the side. Mum had once been very pretty, and Celia looked a great deal like her, in fact, with her mother's soft features, dark wavy hair and pale, freckled skin. But bitterness had hardened Mum's once soft face, forcing its classic Celtic beauty away. "Mum, I'm sorry I disappoint you." She paused, her hand and her insides trembling. "But I love Robert. I want to spend the rest of my life with him."

Mum looked at her. "It would be different if he were the only one, Celia, but they're three, not one. And you haven't forgotten them. I know you. With Donal gone, you'll go back. You'll sin." She turned and put her hands on her hips. "I'll say nothing now because I'm not cruel-hearted. These poor lads have been through enough." She put out a finger at Celia. "But you must look at your life, Celia. Good girls don't behave in certain ways!" At this, she turned sharply around and went back to her cooking, leaving Celia to finish preparing the table in silence.

* * *

After that morning, Celia did what she could to minimize her interaction with her mother, worrying that if she spent too much time in her presence, she would lose her nerve and succumb to her mother's beliefs, the way she had almost three years ago.

She spent as much time as she could with Robert when she wasn't doing her chores, even when he was with his family. She went to Robert every night, making up for all the time they'd spent apart, and for all the loving she had missed. And yet, too often, she scorned herself for how lustful she was, for her seemingly bottomless capacity to climb onto Robert and ride him until her clitoris exploded with orgasms. But Robert did not seem to mind her lusty nature at all, or to think any less of her for it. In fact, since the day he'd come to the Flynn household from the war hospital in England, much of the light had come back into his eyes and his former mischievous life-loving smile now played about his lips the way it always had.

Celia could not deny this change in Robert or her role in it, and she dug deep into her heart, praying on her knees for the strength to remember what was important.

* * *

One Sunday afternoon, almost two weeks later, Celia helped her mother tidy up after dinner and sat outside on the lawn with Robert and Kenneth, enjoying the sunshine. Robert was teasing Celia, poking her ribs and tickling her the way he used to, trying to engage Kenneth in the laughter so that the poor lad might heal a bit from his shell shock.

At first, they were laughing so hard, distracted by Kenneth's gradual participation in their mirth, they didn't hear the motorcar pull up in front of the house. But when the engine went off, Celia, Robert and Kenneth looked up. Lieutenant Graves was there again, going around to the passenger side where another soldier was just opening his door.

Celia felt her pulse quicken and looked at Robert. He looked back at her. "Let's see who it is," he said quietly, reaching for his cane on the grass beside him.

Slowly, they stood, watching the young man get out of the car. He had light brown hair and his eyes were covered with a bandage. Robert and Celia knew him immediately and they went to him as he came up the walk, being led by Lieutenant Graves.

"Patrick," Robert said, "Welcome home, lad."

"Robert!" Patrick whispered. He dropped his pack on the ground and reached out to embrace his old friend. They held onto each other for several moments before Robert released him. "There's someone else here to greet you, Paddy." Robert stepped aside and gently drew Celia forward.

"Hello, Patrick," Celia's eyes filled with tears. Her heart pulsed with joy, and she prayed that Patrick, too, had forgiven her. "Welcome home."

"Celia? Is that you?"

"Aye, it's me. I've missed you so."

Patrick reached up and touched her cheek. "Is it really you?" His lip began to tremble as he felt her skin and hair.

"It's me, Paddy," she said, bursting from joy. His touch told her he had forgiven her, and she took Patrick's hand, pressing it to her lips.

"I've missed you, Ceil." He reached out and pulled her into his arms, letting her wet his jacket with her tears as she held tightly onto him.

Robert picked up Patrick's pack from the ground and Lieutenant Graves suggested they go into the house. Celia linked her arm through Patrick's as they went up the front walk. Robert and the lieutenant walked behind them.

"The mustard gas got me, Ceil," Patrick said sadly. "Thank God my officer was there and got my mask onto me before the shite got into my lungs." He shook his bandaged head. "I'll never be able to see you again. How will I write a poem about your beauty when I can't see it?"

She squeezed his arm tightly to her. "We'll find other ways, Paddy. I swear we will."

At that, Robert gently clasped his hand on Patrick's shoulder. "Believe me, friend," he said in his old mischievous way. "You can take Celia at her word on that." He smiled his lopsided grin as they made their way up the front steps.

* * *

That night before bed, Celia took her bath. Though she tried to relax in the hot rose-scented water, her blood coursed through her entire body. Both Robert and Patrick would be waiting for her in their room, and her stomach fluttered with a mixture of anticipation and anxiety. She was never without her mother's stern visage hovering in her consciousness, judging, and she knew that if it weren't for the long harsh experience of loneliness that had plagued her since she had run from her three friends and their need for her love now, she might have run again.

Celia released a deep sigh and took the washcloth, dipping it in the water and soaping it. She smoothed the cloth all over her body, under her arms and breasts, and between her legs. The brush of the cloth in that sensitive spot made delicious memories flood in.

Several times over the past two weeks, Robert had had her straddle his face so he could pleasure her with his mouth. It had been so long since a man had done that to her that the first time Robert's tongue touched her sweet spot, she had nearly fainted from ecstasy. She'd been glad for being clean and sweet-smelling down there, and made sure she was each night before going to him.

The thought of Robert's face between her thighs stirred her womb. But now Patrick was there as well. Quickly, she rinsed off and stepped out of the tub, drying and powdering herself. Then she put on her nightgown and wrap and brushed her long, wavy hair.

When she went into Robert and Patrick's room, they were waiting for her on the floor. Robert had taken the blankets and pillows off the beds and window seat, making a comfortable cozy spot for them. The sight of Robert and Patrick bare-chested in their pajama bottoms sent a frisson of arousal through her body, and she felt her nipples tighten under her gown. Like Robert, Patrick had a healthy mat of soft sandy-colored hair on his chest, the dusting reaching up to his collarbone and covering his chest muscles, all the way 'round his small tawny nipples. His stomach, too, was hard and flat, with a thin trail of hair plunging to the waistband of his pajamas.

As she went toward them, she felt a strange mixture of arousal and nervousness.

Robert smiled up at her and reached out his hand. "Come, Celia. Your pleasure is doubled tonight."

She took Robert's hand and went down on her knees between the two men. Patrick leaned toward her and put his hand on her arm, gently feeling the thin material of her wrap over her skin. Robert, too, leaned in and nuzzled her cheek and hair. Her stomach fluttered wildly as their combined masculine scents, bay rum aftershave and man, invaded her. In her bewilderment she looked up at Robert, whose eyes were dusky with arousal. "I don't know where to start," she said softly.

Robert put his fingertips under her chin and kissed her lips tenderly. "We start by finding a way to help Paddy see your beauty again and write the poems he really loves. He's probably written enough trench poetry to last many lifetimes. Haven't you, mate?"

Patrick, whose eyes were still hidden underneath his bandage, nodded as he entwined his trembling fingers into Celia's dark hair. "Aye," he answered sadly. "I long to write about Celia again."

She turned to Patrick, feeling a bit bolder. She reached up and touched his cheek just below the large bandage, sliding her fingertips down the clean-shaven plane and across his full, soft lower lip. "You'll write all the poetry in your heart," she murmured, letting the pad of her index finger trace the handsome cleft in his chin.

Robert leaned in toward them. "What did I tell you, Paddy? She's our lass again, for good and all." He moved his large strong farmer's hands sensually up her arms and took hold of her wrap, slipping it off, exposing her soft, freckled skin. He leaned down and kissed her, his lips brushing the tender skin on the side of her neck. Feathers of heat spiraled from his lips.

The tension drained rapidly from Celia's body, leaving her heady and languid from Robert's touch and kiss. Her breathing grew heavier, her body sagging now.

Robert lifted her nightgown over her head, the soft material whispering against her skin as he left her naked between him and Patrick. He took Patrick's hand and placed it palm down on her chest, just above her right breast. The touch jolted her into awareness, his callused fingers trembling on her skin, causing her nipple to tingle and pebble. "Bring me into your senses, love," she whispered to Patrick. "Your heart will give you the words."

Patrick's breathing grew ragged and he began to explore her softly, tenderly, brushing the fingertips of both hands over her chest, down to her breasts, which he cupped in his palms. His breath caught. "They're so soft," he whispered. Gently, almost reverently, he squeezed them, brushing his thumbs over the nipples, then rolling them to stiffness between his fingertips.

Celia's eyes fluttered closed under Patrick's touch and she tilted her head back. Robert captured her lips in soft, deep kisses, tasting her lips and teeth and tongue. She felt a hand on her back, laying her down on the blankets with her head on a pillow. Patrick lay down beside her and began suckling her breast while his other hand began to explore the softness of her stomach. Robert was still kissing her and now fondled her other breast. She moaned, arching her back to push her breast deeper into his seeking hand, overwhelmed by the pleasurable sensations as she entwined her fingers in their hair.

Robert reached down between her thighs and slipped several fingertips inside her warm pink folds. He found her very wet and open, and gathered her musk on his fingertips. He raised his head from kissing her and put his fingertips to his nose, breathing in her scent, then tasting it. "Our goddess' nectar has risen, Paddy," he said softly. He reached down and slid his fingertips into her swollen aching passage sheath, gathering some more of her cream. Sensuously, he smoothed it on her nipple, making the hardened tip exquisitely sensitive to his touch. "Sweeter than wine," he went on. "More potent than the finest Irish whiskey." He grasped Patrick's wrist and brought his hand down onto the dark curls of Celia's mound. "Go down and take a long drink," he told his friend. "That will restore your poetry. It's done wonders for me." Then he leaned down and put his lips close to her ear. "Would you like that, Ceil?"

Celia caught her breath. "Aye," she breathed, letting her legs fall open.

Patrick's hand was trembling on her mound, his fingertips gingerly raking through her springy curls. Slowly, tortuously, he made his way down, feeling the lips of her sex before sliding his fingers inward to the swollen moistness.

He groaned, his fingertips pushing in deeper. "Oh, Ceil. Ohhh." As if suddenly possessed by hunger, Patrick spread open her vaginal lips and lowered his face between her thighs, sealing his lips against her inner sex.

The jolt of heat from his mouth on her pussy spread all the way up to her breasts. She moaned, her sound swallowed by Robert's kiss. She reached up and caressed his dark soft hair as he kissed her and moved down to her breast, licking and suckling it.

The sweet, wild intensity of Robert's mouth on her breasts and Patrick's warm, wet tongue between her legs brought her to bliss, and an orgasm exploded in her swollen clitoris, causing her to tremble and moan as the tiny waves spilled through her.

Patrick circled his tongue around the quivering bud until every last sensation had passed through her. He then raised his face, panting, his chin gleaming with her musk. "Can I have you, Ceil?"

"Aye, please," she breathed just before Robert reclaimed her lips.

Patrick slid down his pajama bottoms. His cock sprang out, thick and hard, a glistening drop of moisture beading at the tiny opening. Lowering his body onto hers, he nestled himself between her spread legs, sliding his cock easily into her swollen wetness.

She moaned again as he moved up, burying himself until the base of his shaft was against her. "Oh, God!" he whispered, his words followed by several short, heavy breaths. He began thrusting fast and wildly, obviously lost in pleasure.

She threw her head back, grabbing onto his buttocks, the hard muscles flexing with his thrusting motions.

Robert had stopped kissing her to watch. At Patrick's fevered thrusting and panting he smiled and looked down at her. "You're his first, Ceil," he whispered.

Her eyes flew open and she and looked up at Robert. "I am?"

Robert leaned down and kissed her. "Couldn't you tell?"

She looked at Patrick, catching her breath as his erection ground against her sweet spot. "No," she answered breathlessly.

Robert grinned. "Go on," he whispered. "Make him as happy as you make me." He lay down beside her, watching, his head propped on his elbow.

Happy to obey, she put her arms around Patrick, pulling him against her, grinding her hips in rhythm to his thrusts. She kissed him deeply, her tongue sliding against his, her hands clutching the wiry muscles of his back. God, he felt so good inside her, his hardness against her slippery tightness. She clenched her vaginal muscles around his cock, wrenching a groan from him that vibrated into her mouth.

He thrust faster, and it was not long before his body trembled in the release of climax, pulsing his warm seed into her.

Still inside her, Patrick collapsed over her, breathing heavily. "I see you again, Celia!" he whispered. "I see you again!" And then he started to cry, burying his face into her neck and hair.

Hot tears in her eyes, she stroked his hair and back, lying quietly beneath him. She smiled at the blissful peace inside her. She felt herself to be the most fortunate lass in the world.

Robert smoothed back her hair, his dark gaze locking with hers. "You see, Ceil," he said gently. "You're our first love."

Her tears crowded her eyes and she put her arms around Patrick, who clung to her, his face still buried in her hair. She turned and kissed his forehead above his bandage while Robert touched her breast. He was still aroused and lay alongside her, his erection pressed against her thigh.

She became aware of Robert's need and kissed him, slipping her hand into his pajama bottoms to stroke his hard cock, her fingertips registering the differences in shape and size to Patrick's. Each man was so special.

Robert closed his eyes and moaned under her touch.

"Patrick," Robert whispered, "May I borrow Celia for a few minutes? We won't be long."

Patrick lifted his head. "Of course," he replied, rolling onto his side.

Robert slipped down his pajama pants and laid back so she could straddle him.

She climbed on, smiling down at him as she slid down the length of his erection to the base. She rocked him, squeezing and grinding against him, feeling the way his particular thickness touched different spots inside her. In moments, the heat re-ignited and her grinding against the base of his cock sent shudders of delight through her womb. In the throes of her orgasm, she squeezed his cock tightly, riding him hard.

"Oh, Ceil!" He groaned, his large hands anchoring her in place, his cock twitching, pulsing in that way it did just before he spilled himself. She grinned down at him and leaned over, thrusting her hips in several short motions. He groaned and climaxed, spilling his seed into her.

She kissed him as he moaned, closing her lips over his, his tongue resting against hers impassively while his body thrummed from his climax.

When the tremors of release had passed, she rested on him for several minutes, stroking his hair before pulling off him so she could lie between him and Patrick. Robert reached beside him and picked up a clean handkerchief, which he pressed to the opening of her vagina. "To catch the excess," he told her.

She looked up at him, thinking for the first time of the possibility that his or Patrick's seed could take root. What if it did and they didn't want a child? Suddenly she became afraid.

Robert saw her expression and gently touched her stomach. "Don't worry, Ceil," he told her, as if he'd read her mind. "We'll be very happy if a babe comes. Won't we, Paddy?"

Patrick had been snuggled against her, playing with a lock of her hair against his cheek while he caressed her bare skin. He leaned over and pressed a kiss onto her shoulder. "Aye. Each of us will want one with you, Ceil."

She lay back and smiled, joyful with relief. "I'd love that." But then her smile faded and she looked at Robert. "But we don't have Freddie back yet. I want to know where he is."

Robert finished wiping her and himself and put the handkerchief aside. Then he lay down next to her and pulled the blanket up over the three of them. He and Patrick snuggled her between them, their muscular bodies warm and musky from sex.

Robert reached out and ruffled Patrick's hair affectionately. "I'm going to phone Freddie's da again tomorrow," he told them. "By now there might be word."

Freddie's father, John Dylan, owned the haberdashery on the main street of Ballykillmarrick, across from Patrick's parents' pub. Robert and Celia had spoken to him several times, but as far as Mr. Dylan knew, Freddie was still at the front.

"I hope so," she whispered, grateful that at least two of them were here with her. That was a million times more than many other people had, including her mother.

Celia kissed them both and closed her eyes, reveling in the feeling of being surrounded by maleness. She breathed in the masculine scents of shaving soap and sexual musk they gave off. If she hadn't been tired already from cooking and cleaning and loving Patrick and Robert all in one day, she might have been tempted to ask for more.

The only thing that left her feeling incomplete was her fear of her mother. Mum had been forbearing with her for the last two weeks for the lads' sakes. But the woman's true feelings would explode sooner or later, and the prospect haunted Celia who worried she would succumb in spite of the lessons she'd learned.

"God bless you, Celia," she heard Robert whisper behind her. He stroked her hair. "Our bodies were damaged. But your love is helping to heal our souls."

Patrick, who had been nuzzling her hair, pressed another kiss on her bare, freckled shoulder. "I love you, Celia."

Her eyes flooded with tears again. "I love you both so much. More than my own life." She squeezed her eyes shut. Please, God, she prayed inside. Make me strong and brave! For love! Then she lay quietly, listening to Robert and Patrick's gentle breathing until she was able to fall asleep.

Chapter Five

The following morning, Dr. Flanagan, who ran the medical clinic in town, came for his weekly visit to examine Robert and Patrick. For Kenneth, the psychiatric doctor was due the next day to have a look at him and determine his readiness to go home.

After the doctor had seen to Robert, who, he reported, was healing better than expected, Robert phoned Freddie's father. Celia stood by, anxiously studying Robert's face for his reactions. Robert saw her and gestured that he'd tell her in a moment what Mr. Dylan was saying.

When Robert had rung off, she grasped his arm. He looked at her and touched her hand gently. "The good news is he's on his way to Scotland," he told her. "And his body is sound."

She tempered her growing excitement when she saw the mixed expression on Robert's face. "And?"

Robert leaned in closer to her ear. "And he's shell-shocked," he whispered.

Her shoulders slumped and she covered her face, stifling a sob. "Why Scotland?" she asked softly.

"They're taking him to Edinburgh," Robert went on. "There's a war hospital there for shell-shocked lads. Craiglockhart, it's called. Freddie's da didn't know anything more than that."

She leaned against the phone table and Robert squeezed her arm. "We'll go to him," he told her softly. "When we know he's there. When he sees you again, he'll heal."

She threw her arms around Robert, grateful for his strength and the inner direction that always seemed to guide him. "Poor Freddie," she whispered.

Robert reached up and stroked her hair. "Just thank God the lad's alive and not maimed," he told her gently, in almost a fatherly way. "With Him, all things are possible."

She looked up at him. "You didn't lose your faith, did you? Even after all that?" Robert smiled. "I almost did," he answered. "But how could I when I came back here and you were restored to me?"

She began to cry and buried her face in his chest while he caressed her hair and placed a tender kiss on the top of her head.

"We must learn to be peaceful people, Celia. Otherwise, what we went through down there in that hell will have been for nothing."

She nodded, wiping her eyes before she soaked Robert's white shirt with her tears.

After several minutes, Robert gently held her away. "Come, Ceil. Let's see what the doc has to say about Paddy."

* * *

The mood of the afternoon was a mixture of sadness and celebration. As with all matters of human existence, the joy of love and reunion was tempered with the knowledge that Robert would always limp, Patrick would never regain his sight, and the damage to Freddie's mind had yet to be known. And, she thought sadly, her relationship with her mother might never be warm and loving.

But the three friends still chose to count their blessings, and their choice enabled them to enjoy each other's company on the front lawn that afternoon, along with Kenneth, after the midday meal. Of course, Robert teased and poked Celia mercilessly, only it was worse now that he had one of his former helpers. Robert held Celia down on the blanket for Patrick to tickle, and though Patrick couldn't see her, he could feel well enough to find her most ticklish spots and set her squealing, just like in the old days.

"Celia Flynn!"

Patrick's hands froze on Celia's sides and Celia lay still, the harsh voice making her heart lurch. She felt the horrid absence of Robert and Patrick near her on the grass, seeing them scramble to their feet. Quickly, she, too, stood up, smoothing down her skirt, running a hand over her hair, her cheeks burning under Mum's flashing eyes, her mum's lips pinched tightly together. Her eyes came to rest on her daughter. "I need you inside. Now."

Celia followed her mother back into the house, feeling the eyes of the three men on her back. She glanced over her shoulder, seeing Robert look at Patrick.

"Is Celia in trouble?" she heard Patrick ask.

Robert put his hand on Patrick's shoulder. "I pray not, lad," he answered.

In the kitchen, Mum turned on her. "What do you think you're doing?" she hissed.

A jolt of prickly fear skittered through Celia's skin. "What do you mean, Mum?" She gripped the back of one of the kitchen chairs to steady her trembling. "We were just playing."

Her mother's eyes flashed. "Is that what you call it now?" she said tightly. "You think I don't know what you do with those lads? Right under my roof?"

Celia's cheeked burned violently with shame. "I love them. They mean my life to me."

Mum narrowed her eyes. "You're a spectacle, you know. Everyone in Ballykillmarrick knows that Celia Flynn is nothing but a --"

"Mrs. Flynn..." Robert's voice came from the doorway with the sternness and authority of a man much older than twenty-three. The sound cut Mum's words off completely, and she turned, along with Celia, to see Robert and Patrick in the doorway to the kitchen, watching them.

Robert's handsome features looked stern. "Please don't say anything you'll regret." He hobbled a few steps into the kitchen and Patrick went with him, guided by his hand on Robert's shoulder.

"I'm speaking with my daughter," Mum told him.

"Your daughter has been an angel of mercy." Robert ignored her. "In spite of how it may appear to you."

"Aye, Mrs. Flynn," Patrick said. "I'd lost my will to live. Celia's helping me to get it back."

Mum turned to Robert and Patrick. "How can you expect me to accept this...this...I don't even know what to call it."

"Love," Robert finished for her. He sighed. "I suppose we can't expect you to. But we can promise you we love Celia and we'll do our best to take care of her and cherish her. She was our first love. We all knew it a long time ago, and we made a promise, Freddie, Patrick and I, that we wouldn't fight over her or tear at her with jealousy, or make her choose between us. God willing, we'll keep our word. We don't ever want to hurt her."

Mum looked down. Some of the harshness had drained from her face and sat heavily in a chair by the kitchen table. "I need Celia to do some errands," she muttered, the hard edge still in her voice. She turned to Celia. "The list is here on the table."

Celia feeling torn by her guilt in the face of Paddy and Robert's incredible love, grabbed up the list and snatched her hat and purse from a peg on the wall, rushing for the kitchen door.

"Celia, wait!" Robert stopped her with his voice as he had her mother. He limped toward her. Patrick stayed with him. When he reached her, he put a hand on her shoulder. "Promise me you'll come right back when you're finished. Give me your word."

She looked at him, her lower lip trembling. She saw fear and worry in his eyes, and realized that though he'd forgiven her the past, the result of her having run away had had its effect. He could not fully trust her. Nor could Patrick. The knowledge sliced her heart painfully, more so than her mother's harsh words. She had to do something to regain their trust. The pain in Robert's eyes, pain she'd caused, was unbearable. "I promise, Robert. I give you my word." She reached up and put her hand on his cheek, not caring now that her mother was a few feet away. She kissed him and Patrick and went out the door.

* * *

Walking through the town, Celia had to fight back constant tears. *Why does it have to be so hard?* she thought sadly. What would she do if her mother hated her for the rest of their lives? Why had God made her the way He had? Why couldn't she be like other girls and fall in love with one man and marry him and have children, and not cause such problems?

The center of town was bustling, and Celia found she craved some quiet place where she could think. She kept walking, following the road that went to Dublin. She wound around a large hill towering above the rocky coast and wandered to the side of the road, making her way down the grassy hillside, in the direction of the rocks. But the footing was growing steep and dangerous, so she decided to sit and look out at the sea.

All the while her mother's sharp words rang in her mind. Thank God Robert had stopped Mum from saying what she had been about to say. Celia could only imagine what her mother had been about to call her. Whatever word she had chosen would have made Celia feel even more low and filthy. She began to cry and looked down at the rocks far below.

Robert and Patrick had been so loving, defending her the way they had. She didn't deserve such loyalty and respect. They were the best of men. But even Robert's moving speech had not made a dent in her mother's heart. Celia began to feel hopelessly trapped. She watched the foamy water crash and break over the rocks far below her. A terrible thought came to her mind. She had promised Robert she would come back after doing her errands. He had been afraid she'd run away again. But what if she fell? She couldn't run away then. Her mother wouldn't have to worry about the reputation of the Flynn family anymore. And Celia wouldn't have to be torn by this horrible guilt.

"That's not the answer, Celia," she heard a man's voice say behind her.

Celia turned and looked up. A man was standing there. He had dark hair under his cap, a small moustache and blue eyes. He wore a heavy moss-stitch sweater and trousers. She looked closely at him. She knew him. It was…It couldn't be! Her heart shuddering, she closed her eyes. When she opened them, he was still there, puffing his pipe, watching her. The sweater was one Mum had made for him, and he had been wearing it the last time Celia saw him alive. "Da?" she said in disbelief.

Tom Flynn chuckled. "Aye, it's me. Sort of."

Celia stood up, carefully making her way toward him.

"Careful, Celia," he warned. "I can't grab you if you fall."

But Celia made her way to safe footing and stopped in front of him. "Da, you look…so…alive!"

Her father chuckled again. "I look how you want me to look, love."

She blinked again, expecting him to disappear. But he didn't. "Are you real?"

Tom Flynn puffed his pipe. "Real enough. You need me now, so I'm here."

She sighed and her shoulders sagged, her grief overwhelming her joy and disbelief. "You were always there when I had problems with Mum."

"This is more than that, Celie," he said softly. "You were thinking of ending your life. I couldn't have that. Nor could those lads."

Celia looked at her father's image before her. "You aren't ashamed of me?"

Her father smiled. "No, love, I'm not ashamed. But even if I were, that's my problem, not yours. In this life, you accept love when it's offered, no matter how strange it seems."

She held out her hands in a pleading gesture. "But I'm so very strange, Da! God made a mistake!"

"God doesn't make mistakes, Celia." Her father waved his pipe. "He made you for a purpose. A good one. Haven't the lads made that clear enough to you? Or are you as stubborn as your mum?"

Celia started crying again. "I don't want to end up bitter like she is," she said through her tears.

Tom Flynn took a puff on his pipe. "Then accept yourself the way you are. I know it's easy for me to say and hard for you to do, especially when your mum stands there, hands on hips, eyes flashing like the devil himself." He pointed. "You must remind yourself that it's her own fears talking, not the truth." He sighed. "How different Margaret's life would have been if she had accepted *herself.* I tried to tell her this, you know." He shook his head sadly. "She wouldn't listen."

Celia wiped at her tears. "Aye, I know you did, Da." She watched him a moment. "I feel better. Thanks."

Her father regarded her, his blue eyes soft with the affection she always remembered. "Thank God. I couldn't have withstood something terrible happening to you." He smiled and puffed his pipe. "You've got a little one to think of now as well," he added after a moment.

Her heart jumped and she sat up straighter. "Do you mean...?"

Tom Flynn nodded. "Aye," he answered. "But you already knew that, didn't you? You can't go at it like jackrabbits and not have a babe to show for it now, can you?"

She blushed. "Da!" But she had always loved her father's humor and laughed. However, her mirth passed and she grew serious. "It's Robert's, isn't it?"

Her father chuckled. "Aye. But you knew that too. It seems only right. He's sort of the leader, isn't he? The alpha wolf, so to speak. In zoological terms, that is."

She smiled. "I didn't know you knew anything about zoology, Da."

He looked at her, his eyes sad. "There's a lot I didn't get to tell you. We didn't have enough time, you and I, Ceil. A shame. We had what it takes to be good friends."

She returned his sad gaze. "I know. I miss you horribly."

"I miss you, too, love. But the truth is, I'm always right here." He tapped his chest by his heart, then smiled and puffed his pipe. "Now, you go back. Do your errands and go home to your lads."

She smiled back at him, feeling strengthened the way she always had after one of their talks. "Aye, Da. I love you."

Tom Flynn smiled and took his pipe from between his teeth. "I love you, little one," he answered.

Celia turned and made her way carefully up to the road, sensing her father at her side. But when she looked up, he was gone. She scanned the road in front of her for him, but he wasn't there. She sighed as a pang of missing him passed through her. But then she remembered all he'd told her and smiled, peaceful for the first time that day as she headed back toward town.

As she ran her errands, she thought about the babe growing inside her. Robert's babe. She doubled her pace, now in a rush to get home.

* * *

When Celia got back to the house, she found Robert and Patrick in the living room, sitting quietly, waiting for her. They both stood up the second she walked in. The relief on their faces pained her when she realized how worried they'd been she'd run away again, and she swore to herself to make amends for all the anguish she'd ever caused them. She put down her groceries and went into their embraces. They brought her down to sit between them on the sofa, kissing her, touching her cheeks, holding onto her hands. "I'm sorry," she whispered over and over as they loved her. "I'm so sorry."

"It's all right," Robert whispered back between kisses. "Just don't ever go away again."

"I won't." She kissed him and Patrick on the cheeks and lips. "I promise." She then took each of their hands and put them on her stomach. "Guess what, lads?"

Robert caught his breath. "Celia, are you...?

Celia smiled at him. "Aye," she answered. "Yours is first."

"How did you know so soon?"

"You wouldn't believe me if I told you."

"Try me," Robert said.

So Celia, having great faith in her lovers, told them about her father's visit, leaving out, of course, the part about how she'd been considering a fall off the cliff. Thankfully, Patrick and Robert believed her incredible experience. She then turned to Patrick. "I want one with you too, Paddy," she said softly.

Patrick touched her cheek. "I know. God willing, there's time. I have to learn how to get around without me eyes first."

She smiled and kissed him. Then she rested for a moment with their hands in hers, their fingers interlaced. When the grandfather clock in the front hall struck half-four, however, Celia knew she'd have to go to the kitchen to help her mother prepare supper. Her stomach fluttered nervously at the thought, but then she felt the change inside that her father's visit had wrought in her. He had helped her find self-love, the very thing that would protect her from giving up what was true in her heart. And no matter what anyone thought or felt about her, she did not have to stop loving her three lads. That was up to her.

She rose from the sofa and picked up her groceries.

"By the way," Robert said as she headed toward the kitchen, "Mr. Dylan called while you were out. Freddie's at Craiglockhart now."

She turned and gasped. "Thank God! When can we go see him?"

"I was thinking tomorrow," Robert answered. "As long as your mum has enough help."

She nodded, her heart racing. "I'll work it out with her. We need to go."

Robert nodded and sat back.

In the kitchen, Mum was already at work by the stove. She looked briefly at Celia when she came in, but then turned back around without a word.

Celia laid the groceries on the table and started to put them away, her hands trembling. She watched her mother's back as she worked, waiting for her to turn again and say something, anything. But she didn't. Finally, Celia went over to her. "Mum."

Mum looked at her. "What is it?"

"It's not my fault you gave up your art."

To her surprise, her mother looked afraid rather than angry. "How did you know about that?"

"From Da."

Mum shook her head. "Of course. I should have known. You and he were thick as thieves."

Celia ignored the harsh remark and took a deep breath. "I'm going to need your help and support. I need your love. You could have a houseful of beautiful grandchildren and loving sons. Are you going to be there, or will you let your bitterness drive us away?"

Margaret Flynn looked startled at Celia's tone. She gazed into her daughter's eyes, seeing a different young woman, one who would not be cowed. "You sound just like your father."

Celia squared her shoulders. "I'm glad for that. So, Mum what do you say? Do you love me?"

"Of course I do, Celia. I want you to be happy." She went over to the table and sat down heavily. She sighed, toying with a corner of her apron.

Celia went over to her. "Loving those three lads makes me happy, Mum."

Mum rubbed her forehead, her eyes closed. Celia turned and went back to putting away the groceries. All of a sudden, she heard a sniffle. She looked back and saw her mother rubbing her eyes. She went over to her and put a hand on her shoulder. "Mum?" she asked softly.

Mum mother looked up at her, her eyes red and teary. "I'll try, Celia," she said quietly, obviously struggling to take the edge from her voice.

Celia felt her own tears rise again and squeezed her mother's shoulder. "Thank you, Mum. That's all I ask."

* * *

That night, Celia took her bath and went to Robert and Patrick's room.

They were waiting for her on the floor, like the night before, their pajama tops open, revealing their broad strong chests.

Robert had arranged the blankets and pillows and they held their hands out to her when she approached.

She smiled as she knelt down, her body vibrantly alive with pulsing and throbbing. She hugged them and kissed them with deep passionate kisses. Her body burned for them and she slipped off her wrap and pulled her nightgown over her head.

At the sight of her nakedness, Robert's eyes went dusky and he reached out and gently squeezed one of her breasts, his thumb brushing reverently back and forth across the nipple.

She moaned and her eyes fluttered closed. Then she felt Patrick's hand on her other breast and his lips pressing a soft kiss into the side of her neck. She moaned again as her body weakened and she felt her clit swelling and moistening between her legs.

Robert chuckled softly as he rolled her nipple gently, teasingly between his fingertips. "You hear that, Paddy? Our goddess can't get enough of our love."

Patrick kissed her neck some more, his lips open so his tongue could flicker against her skin teasingly. He squeezed her breast, eliciting another moan from her. "That bodes well for us, doesn't it?"

Robert grinned, his dark eyes glowing with hunger. "Aye." His hand wandered down her stomach, to her mound of dark curls. He caressed her slit, slipping his fingertips into her wet, open passage. "It certainly does."

Hungry to feel his cock, she reached out and pressed her hand against Robert's erection, rubbing in small circles until he, too, moaned. She pulled down his pajama pants, letting his cock spring free, taking the hard shaft into her hand, stroking it. God, how she loved the feel of smooth, warm skin over hard muscle.

She longed to taste it and captured it in her mouth, delighting in the feel of the head pressing against the roof of her mouth. She went down on her hands and knees, her eyes closed, gently sliding her lips up and down Robert's cock. A droplet of seed oozed from the tiny opening and she lapped up the salty sweet moisture.

She felt Patrick's hands on her hips, caressing her. One hand ventured downward, his fingertips spreading her open. Thick fingers probed her wet softness, rubbing her clit and pushing deep into her passage, as if testing her readiness to be fucked.

She moaned, pushing her hips back, seeking to be filled with Patrick's cock, but unable to ask because her lips were still around Robert's.

Patrick seemed to understand, for in the next second, the thrust of his hardness pushed into her, filling her deeply, all the way, until their bodies touched. Her moan of pleasure vibrated around Robert's shaft and Robert gasped, his hips bucking lightly, his large strong fingers winding into her hair.

"Oh, Ceil, lass, don't stop," Robert murmured as she suckled and licked his hard length. His fingers tightened in her hair, gently pushing his cock deeper into her mouth.

Robert's gentle control made her moan deep in her throat. Her mouth and her sheath were filled with men and her senses were heightened, soaring. She felt as if she were entering some heavenly, celestial sphere, and her heart was full, bursting.

She was so rapt with bliss that she didn't know when they had withdrawn and took her in hand, laying her back on the blankets to be pleasured and mounted and loved. Patrick nestled between her legs and she felt his hardness slip inside her, filling her with delicious heat.

With her head thrown back, she caressed his hip and backside, moaning with each hot thrust. When she turned her head, Robert captured her mouth with his, suckling furiously on her tongue, plunging recklessly into the deep recesses of her mouth with possessive fervor.

Patrick's body shuddered and Celia felt his warm seed spilling out inside of her. He collapsed gently on her, panting, but after a moment, he rolled to the side so she could rise and mount Robert. Her sheath was so wet and swollen she slid easily onto him and rode away as he'd taught her to do, her own body shuddering with release twice before she brought him to climax.

She collapsed over him, resting her cheek on his shoulder. Reaching out, she caressed Patrick's hair tenderly. He grasped her wrist and placed a small kiss on the tender skin.

"Just think," Robert breathed, his breath becoming normal again. "Tomorrow, we'll all be together again."

She sighed. "I can only hope Freddie's forgiven me as you two have."

Robert's hand was warm and gently, caressing her bare back. "Freddie's a gentle lad, Ceil. He's always told me how much he missed ye." He pressed a kiss into her neck. "Just wait, you'll see. Tomorrow, ye'll be complete again."

Robert's words brought tears to her eyes, and she prayed he was right.

Chapter Six

Celia's heart pounded as she, Robert and Patrick mounted the steps to Craiglockhart. They'd traveled all the preceding day on the ferry over to Scotland and then the train to Edinburgh. By the time they'd taken a room at an inn on Prince's Street, it had been too late in the evening to visit Freddie.

Now, in the mid-morning sun, the large stone building gleamed ominously. It had once been part of a beautiful lordly estate, surrounded by green lawns and shrubberies. But Celia saw it only as the place that held her dear Freddie, the last stop between his coming home or going back to war.

Robert squeezed her hand. "Don't worry, Ceil," he told her with a gentle smile, "It'll all come out all right."

Patrick's hand tightened on her shoulder. "Aye, Celie, we'll all be together again."

She suppressed her tears and went through the door that Robert held open for her. Patrick still held her shoulder, letting her guide him.

Her heart thudded inside her like a jackrabbit caught in a bag. The airy front hall with dark paneled walls and a black and white tiled floor felt like an eerie combination of a somber hospital and Scottish laird's estate. She fought the urge to call out for Freddie, wondering where in this huge, gothic place he could possibly be.

Thank God for Robert, who did all the talking to the receptionist. "Aye," she heard him say to the uniformed man at the desk, they were here to see Freddie Dylan of Ballykilmarrick. No, they weren't family. A pang of sadness gripped her heart. Mr. Dylan had refused to come see his son, declaring Freddie's condition a symptom of being yellow. What a horror it had been to hear him say such a thing about his own son. He'd always mistaken Freddie's penchant for mathematics and intellect as a sign of physical cowardice. But Freddie was anything but a coward.

"We'd like to see him all the same," Robert told the man. "We're his family for what it's worth. They won't come here to see him."

The man cleared his throat and rose from the desk. "I'll get a VAD to fetch him for you."

Robert nodded with an air of authority. "Thank you."

Celia's arm remained link through Robert's and she pressed in closer to him. She stared at the doorway through which the receptionist had gone and come back out, telling them that Freddie would be down momentarily.

Beside her, Patrick stood, his hand still on her shoulder. "Do you see him?" he asked softly.

Her heart hammered. "Not yet." No sooner had she spoken, however, than she saw a flash of golden hair as the door swung open. The young man walking out in his officer's uniform was Freddie, but for the pasty complexion and haunted expression that dulled the blue of his eyes.

A VAD led Freddie over to them. She smiled gently as she released him. "Here are your friends, Lieutenant Dylan."

Freddie's arms remained at his sides. He stood quietly, staring at them, his gazing roving over their faces.

Celia squeezed Robert's arm, afraid to rush at Freddie, lest she startle him. She remembered poor Kenneth Neary and forced a smile. "Hi, Freddie. God, I'm so happy to see you."

"Hey, lad," Robert said gently, reaching a tentative hand to Freddie's shoulder.

Freddie looked at him, a faraway look in his eyes.

"Why don't you take him into the day room?" the VAD said. "You can sit down and someone will come round with tea."

"Thank you." Celia reached gently for Freddie's hand. Her heart ached at the way he let her lead him, like a child, into the large dayroom.

Comfortable looking sofas and chairs lined the edges of the large room, in the center of which stood a tennis table and more tables with card decks. Men sat at some of the tables while other soldiers, some looking as emotionally wounded and haunted as Freddie, sat in various places, either talking quietly or staring out at the cloudy summer day through the tall windows. The room had evidently once served as an elegant ballroom. However, now no one was dancing or laughing.

Celia ushered Freddie to one of the sofas and sat down next to him while Robert brought Patrick to sit on his other side and took a chair across from them for himself. She looked up at Robert, fighting back tears. "Doesn't he remember us?"

Robert nodded, his brow creased. "Aye, of course he does. Don't' ye, lad? He isn't completely back yet."

She held Freddie's hand between both of hers, not knowing what to say.

"Come on then, Freddie," Robert urged gently. "You're among friends now. Paddy and I both know what you've been through." He reached over and ruffled Freddie's golden hair. "Talk to us."

Freddie's lower lip trembled and his eyes clouded to a shade of gray. "I told the dreams I wouldn't talk to them," he murmured.

"Dreams, Freddie?" Patrick said. "This isn't a dream, lad. We're really here."

Freddie shook his head. "Nay, Celia is a dream."

She gasped softly and squeezed his hand. "No, Freddie. I'm here."

He looked at her. "You left."

"She's come back, Freddie," Robert said. "She even gave her mum a what-for, lad. She won't be lettin' anyone else tell her who to love."

She put a hand on his shoulder. She ached to put her arms around him. "Freddie, I'm so sorry. I've missed you horribly. Please forgive me."

Freddie reached his hand to her cheek, brushing his fingertips tentatively over her skin. His blue eyes misted, churning with a look of disbelief, as if she might vanish suddenly. "You're really here," he breathed.

"Like I told you, Ceil," Robert interjected, "he's already forgiven you. Nothing we're saying right now is getting in. All that matters to him is that you love him. Believe me, I know."

She reached up, eyes blurred with tears and put her hand on Freddie's shoulder. As soon as she did, he leaned forward, pulling her into his arms.

His face pressed into the side of her neck and his back trembled under her hands.

She closed her eyes and squeezed him in her arms, smoothing her palm across his back over his uniform jacket. "It's all right, Freddie, love," she crooned.

Freddie's fingertips dug into her back through her jacket. His body was warm against hers. Tears burned in her eyes as the sweetness of holding her long lost friend washed through her.

"What do you say, mates, we get out of here?" Robert said after a few moments. "Best thing for Freddie now is a pint with his friends and then some time to get reacquainted with his girl."

Celia looked up at Robert. "Is he allowed to leave here?"

"Of course he is. This ain't a prison, for however much it feels like one. I'm going to tell them he's staying with us." Robert rose from the sofa, leaning heavily on his cane.

* * *

In a pub on Prince's Street, Celia sat in the corner of the booth with Freddie on one side of her and Robert and Patrick on the other side. Around them was the murmuring, laughter and clinking of glass one heard in a pub.

The waiter brought them drinks and took their order for a meal.

When he'd gone, Robert raised his glass. "Here's to us being together again. Our separation was long and bitter, but it's made our reunion that much sweeter."

"Hear hear," Patrick said, taking a hearty swig from his glass.

Freddie sipped quietly and set his glass down. "Does me da know I'm here?" he asked just loudly enough to be heard over the sounds of the crowded pub.

Celia looked at Robert who frowned.

"Aye, Freddie, he does," Robert answered gently.

Freddie bowed his head, seeming to stare into his glass. "He's not coming to see me, is he?"

Celia squeezed Freddie's hand.

"No, laddie," Robert answered. "I'm sorry."

Freddie nodded. "I'm sure I know what he said. That I'm yellow, eh?" He sighed. "When Ceil left, he said it was probably because not one of us three was man enough to stake his claim on her. He says what kind of windy fuckwit is it what lets two other blokes knock the hole off his bird?"

"An intelligent bloke, that's who," Robert said immediately. He grinned, his dark eyes sparkling mischievously.

"That's right," Patrick chimed in. "If one of us is going to get yelled at for pissin' the bowl, we can point the finger at the other two. Two more blokes to share the blame."

"Paddy's got it right," Robert said. "And we all know that one lass is too much for any one bloke to handle anyhow. Easier on our poor overused pipes to pass her around between us." He and Patrick laughed heartily.

"You two!" Celia said, but she joined in the laughter. When her gaze fell on Freddie, he was watching her. A sheen of hunger blazed in the depths of his eyes, causing her to fall silent.

Before she knew what was happening, Freddie cupped the back of her neck and took her mouth in a hot kiss.

Her eyes fluttered closed and she surrendered to the kiss. Cheers and clapping sounded around them, and she suspected they were meant for her and Freddie, but the world around them receded when his tongue slipped between her lips, tasting her with mounting passion.

"Go fer it, laddie!" Celia heard a man call from the bar. "Ye've earned it!" More cheers followed his statement.

Freddie pressed his lips harder, his tongue slipping between her lips, invading her mouth with delicious heat.

Her eyelids fluttered and she sank back against the hard wood of the bench. Robert was close beside her and she felt him slip his hand surreptitiously under her skirt, stroking her thigh with teasing fingertips. He slid upward, beneath the thin material of her drawers, moving dangerously close to her sex. He skimmed his touch over her lower lips and she pulled away from Freddie's kiss with a gasp.

"What's the matter, Ceil," Robert said in a devilish voice, "A bit jumpy aren't ye?"

She breathed heavily, aroused from Freddie's kiss and from Robert's touch. She struggled to appear calm and nodded. "Aye, a bit jumpy."

He grinned again and patted her knee under the table. "Well, then, I suppose we'll have to get you back to the room and wear you out a bit. You'll calm down, I suspect."

Her breath caught softly. For the first time in over three long years, she was going to be together with her three lads. And this time, she wasn't going to stop them from making love to her.

Chapter Seven

"Here we are." Robert opened the door to their room, "Alone at last." He stood aside for Celia to go in and waited for Freddie and Patrick, who held on to Freddie's shoulder. "It's not our hay pile, but it'll do."

Celia unpinned her hat and set it down. Robert helped her off with her jacket and slung it over the back of a chair.

"Sit ye's down." Robert poured a glass of whiskey. He held it up before Celia, Patrick and Freddie, who were now seated on the sofa by the hearth. "It can't be said enough how grateful I am that the good Lord above saw fit to bring us back together." He took a sip of the whiskey and handed it to Celia.

She sipped from the glass and handed it to Patrick who, in turn, gave it to Freddie. Robert went to the door and locked it. As soon as she saw him turn the lock, her heart set to pounding and her stomach tumbled about. She remembered that afternoon in the hay when the lads had given her the beautiful necklace she still wore. The afternoon that had begun with such sweetness and which she'd made go sour.

"So," Robert cut into her thoughts, "Do we wait for nightfall, or is now the right time?"

Freddie sat up straighter and reached for Celia. "Now is the right time. I want to finish what I started." He leaned over and pressed his lips to hers.

She murmured softly in her throat as she clasped her arms around Freddie, accepting the deliciously hard warmth of his body pressing against hers. Her body softened completely, opening, wanting to take Freddie inside her.

He plundered her mouth with mounting fervor, suckling her tongue, while one hand pulled the pins from her hair, letting it tumble free so he could weave both hands into it. His erection, fully engorged, pressed demandingly through his uniform trousers into her belly and he ground his pelvis against hers, communicating to her his pent-up longing.

Freddie kissed her until she was breathless before he raised his head and looked up at Robert and Patrick. "I'm sorry. I'm hogging her."

"That's no problem, mate," Robert said softly. He stood behind the sofa, close to her. He reached out and caressed her hair, trailing his fingertips across her forehead and down her cheek. He traced the seam of her lips, pushing his fingertip between them.

She moaned and flicked her tongue over the pad of his index finger. He pushed his finger deeper in and she suckled it, her hunger mounting from the massage of his fingertip on the roof of her mouth.

"Our lusty girl has had plenty of me and Paddy these last few weeks. Tonight is for you, Freddie. Whatever ye want." He pulled his finger from Celia's seeking mouth and unbuttoned the top few buttons of her blouse. He separated the material and slid his hand onto her chest, palm down.

His warm skin trailed fire through her body as he massaged the tops of her breasts under her chemise. She moaned softly.

Robert chuckled. "She can never get enough, this lass." He inched his touch down further, grazing her nipples with his sensuous massage.

Patrick was sitting beside her and he felt his way to the front of her blouse, working the rest of the buttons open slowly, one by one. "We'll get her ready for ye, mate. And then she'll be all wet and panting for ye to have her. How's that sound?"

Freddie nodded, his gaze raking hungrily over her exposed skin. "Aye," he breathed, slipping his trembling hands under her skirt, caressing her thighs over her stockings. "I never thought I'd see such loveliness again in me life."

Patrick had finished undoing her blouse and now worked on the fastenings of her skirt. He'd done them enough in the past few weeks that he didn't need his sight for the task. He opened the skirt and Freddie slipped it down her legs, letting it drop to the floor.

Robert leaned over her, gently tilting her face upward so he could kiss her. He slipped his tongue possessively between her lips, laving every soft recess of her mouth while Patrick smoothed his hand across her breasts, squeezing each one gently before pushing the straps of her chemise off her shoulders.

Freddie eased off her slip and leaned over, brushing soft kisses on her thighs where they were exposed between her stockings and her drawers. As he'd done that day so long ago, he trailed his fingertips up her inner thigh, stopping tentatively when he'd reached the area so dangerously close to her lower lips.

She looked up and saw him eyeing her, a tentative expression clouding his blue eyes. His lip trembled and his fingertips thrummed along the supple skin of her inner thigh. "Don't stop, Freddie," she breathed.

She heard his breath hiss softly just before he slid his hand up, gingerly grazing the sensitive outer folds between her thighs. She moaned softly as he continued to explore, skating his fingertips up and down the length of her slit before pushing them gently in between the soft folds.

Freddie found the hard little bud and rubbed it up and down, causing her to cry out softly from the intense pleasure.

Robert caught her cries with a kiss and Patrick suckled harder on her nipple.

Celia's eyelids fluttered closed and she tilted her head back, her body sinking completely into the cushions, a tingling mass of quivering need under three pairs of hands and three mouths.

The next she realized, something warm and moist swiped against her inner sex. Her eyes flew open and she saw Freddie's blond head between her thighs, his mouth tasting her hungrily.

She heaved several ragged breaths as the erotic tension built in her core, like violin strings reverberating from each passionate swipe of the bow across them. "Oh, Freddie," she whispered, curling a hand into his short-cropped golden hair.

Her eyes closed again as the three men worked her body into a froth. When Freddie took her clitoris between his lips and teeth and suckled it, one finger pulsing in and out of her passage, the pleasure sent her over the edge into bliss. Her orgasm erupted under his loving mouth, wave after wave of bliss overtaking her.

Robert absorbed her cries with a deep kiss and she sank down, limp from the intensity.

Freddie lifted his face from between her thighs. He unbuckled his trousers hastily, pulling them and his drawers down. "I can't wait any longer, Celia," he breathed, sliding up between her thighs and finding her moist openness with the head of his erection.

"It's all right, Freddie." She reached for him, stretching her legs apart. She gasped as he slid easily inside her moist cave and lowered his mouth hungrily to hers.

She parted her lips, accepting his tongue, tasting her own tangy cream on his lips.

He plunged his mouth against hers, suckling with fervor on her tongue as he moved rapidly in and out of her, conveying in his fevered movements his pent-up longing for her.

She slid her hands under the loose waist of his trousers, exploring the smooth hard muscles that flexed with his movements, rubbing and squeezing his buttocks, pulling him deeper inside of her.

In moments, Freddie groaned. His body tightened and moved with small jerking motions.

Celia felt his warm seed pulsing into her before he collapsed gently over her, breathing heavily. She smiled and caressed his back, squeezing him tightly in her arms. "Thank God you're home, Freddie," she whispered.

For several moments they lay like that and she saw Robert come from around the back of the sofa and settle into a chair. Patrick sat on the floor, his back to the sofa, his head leaning back against her arm.

"It's all right, Ceil," Robert said, "Patrick and I will have our turn in a bit. Freddie needs this time with you." He smiled at her with love shining in his dark eyes.

She sighed and caressed Freddie's wheat-colored hair. His breathing had calmed somewhat, but he lay quietly with his face pressed into her neck. One hand was closed around her shoulder, holding her as if he couldn't let her get away from him.

She kissed his head and held him close, her happiness marred only by the prospect of Freddie's having to go back to the Front.

The only thing she could do now was enjoy the time they had together.

Chapter Eight

One month later...

It is the assessment of the Medical Board of Craiglockhart War Hospital that Lt. Frederick Dylan continues to suffer a severe case of neurasthenia due to his time spent in active duty on the Front. It is our recommendation that Lt. Dylan be given an honorable discharge from service and be permitted to return home. Dr. Jonathan Rivers, M.D.

Celia read the piece of paper over and over then clasped it to her breast like a precious treasure. Hot tears flowed liberally and the tension drained from her body. Of course, the fact that Freddie often stuttered and had nervous ticks in his eyes that he'd never had before, distressed her. However, these symptoms also meant that he could come home and be with her.

She smiled through her tears at Robert, then at Freddie and Patrick. "Can it really be true?" she asked softly, clutching the paper. "We're going home, all of us together?"

Robert put his hands on her shoulders. "We *are* home, love, as long as we're together." He furrowed his brow. "I've been giving this a lot of thought and I decided that if any gobshite in Ballykill starts in on any one of us because of who we are, I'm packing us up and taking us to Paris."

She stared at him. "France?"

Robert grinned. "Aye. Don't forget, the three of us spent some time down there. The other lads can tell you, just about every man has more than one woman and every woman has more than one man. We'll fit in there better than a curl of wool on a sheep's arse."

She laughed heartily. "You're so funny!"

He smiled and kissed her lips gently, silencing her laughter. "Perhaps so, Ceil, but I'm dead serious. Life's too short to be given all kinds of shite over love. I won't stand for anyone saying hurtful things to the people I love. Any of ye's."

"Aye, Robert's right," Paddy said.

She nodded and leaned over, kissing Patrick softly on the mouth. "Aye, he is."

Robert ruffled his hand through her hair. "Well then, that settles it. It's too late to leave today. We'll go first thing tomorrow." He gently took the paper from her hand and set it aside.

Reflexively, she reached for it, but he held it out of her grasp. "Don't worry, sweetheart," he said, "This is for real.

Freddie doesn't have to go back. You were there when the doc himself told us. In the meantime, however, we have a bit o' celebrating to do."

Her heart skipped lightly and she looked expectantly at Robert who wore his usual mischievous grin. "What is it tonight?" she asked, heart pounding, her body humming already with need.

"Ah, a surprise." He took her hand and led her over to the bed. Freddie followed, along with Patrick who held onto his shoulder. "Now, Ceil, you must disrobe." Robert turned her to face him and began unbuttoning her blouse. The brush of his fingertips against her made her blood pound hotly through her veins.

Freddie's hands slipped around her waist and he undid her skirt, which pooled around her ankles. Sliding his fingers under the waist of her slip, he tugged it down and then did the same with her drawers.

When Robert had gotten her blouse off, Patrick felt his way to her shoulders and lifted off her chemise.

With trembling hands, she undid her garter belt and Freddie slipped her stockings off until she stood in the middle of a pile that had been her clothing. She was naked, surrounded by their appreciative gazes. Her breathing grew ragged from the erotic sensation of being completely exposed to them while they were all still clothed.

Robert picked up one of her scarves that lay on the bed. "We're going to play a little game I invented called Guess Who? He covered her eyes with the scarf and tied it gently but firmly into place as he spoke. "The object of the game is to guess which lad is which simply by touch."

Her body heated several more degrees and she caught her breath softly.

Robert released her hand and she heard the soft sounds of clothing being unbuttoned and unfastened around her. "There's only one rule, Ceil," he went on. "No touching the face. Keep it between the neck and the..." He chuckled. "Nether regions."

"What happens if I guess all three correctly?"

"That's simple. If ye win, ye get all three of us to fill you up at once."

Her breath hitched as a jolt of heat sliced through her body.

"Aye," Robert went on. "Through the back door, the front door, and the roof."

"Robert's a sweet talker, ain't he?" Patrick quipped.

Freddie snickered.

"Aye, that's me," Robert said in a silky voice.

Her nipples tingled wildly and her sex pulsed with the heat his silky voice and erotic suggestions were sending into her body. "And if I lose?"

Robert chuckled softly. "If ye lose, lass, you get a spanking from each one of us before we fill you up."

She could not suppress the moan that escaped her. "It seems I win either way," she said.

"Aye, Celia. So do we." He said, brushing a hand lightly over her breasts. His touch was tender as usual and the sensual rasp of his callused skin against her nipples made her sigh deeply.

"As soon as we get onto the bed with ye, ye can begin." He picked up her hand. "Come here, onto the bed," he said, guiding her onto the bed in a kneeling position on the center of the mattress. All around her, the mattress sank with the weight of Robert, Patrick and Freddie climbing onto the large bed. The sounds of their ragged breathing and the male scent and heat of their bodies surrounded her.

Celia rose up on her knees and reached out, guided toward whomever was in front of her by the sound of his aroused breathing. Her hands landed on hard, warm muscle that quivered under her touch. She brushed her fingertips over the crisp-soft chest hair and explored the hard slopes. She smiled. There was no mistaking this broad chest and work-hardened physique. She slid her hand down his stomach, following the trail of hair that led to his erection, which she grasped lightly and began to stroke. She heard him stifle the sharp intake of breath as she slid her hand along the smooth shaft and down to cup his heavy balls. "This is Robert, for sure," she said softly.

"Aye." His hands went to her shoulders, caressing them in small circles. "Give me pipe a lick, would ye, Ceil?"

She nodded and dappled a trail of kisses down his chest and stomach, breathing in his unique musky scent. Bending her face to his cock, she swiped the swollen head with a gentle tongue.

"Ahhh, thank you," he breathed.

She rose up and turned to where she heard someone breathing. Reaching out, her hands brushed a pair of strong shoulders. She slid her fingertips down his arms, feeling each definition of hard muscle. She felt his hands, strong yet gentle hands. She lifted one of them to her lips and touched her tongue to the pads of his fingertips. The skin was warm and pleasantly salty.

"This is Patrick," she said softly.

"Are ye certain of that, lass?" Robert said, always the devil.

She smiled. "Of course I am."

He chuckled and grasped her wrist, guising her hand through the air. "Just check the third one to be absolutely sure."

Her hand landed on a smooth plane of muscle before Robert released her. Left free to explore, she smoothed her hand across the male chest, recognizing Freddie's slim yet sinewy musculature, the soft hair of his chest brushing pleasantly against her fingertips. "Aye," she said, "I was right. This is Freddie." Her other hand still rested on Patrick's chest, which she brushed with eager fingertips. "This is Patrick."

Robert laughed. "Well done, Ceil. You won the game. Time for yer spanking."

A shivery tingle passed through her body. "Spanking? But I won."

Robert's strong arms closed gently around her and he maneuvered her onto her hands and knees. "I changed me mind. I made the game. I can change the rules." He smoothed his hand over the globes of her buttocks, his callused hands grazing the soft flesh with the most erotic friction.

Though she still wore the blindfold, Celia could feel Patrick and Freddie closing in around her, their breathing ragged in her ears, their body heat warming her own skin. The air around her was redolent with the scent of male musk.

"Ready, lads?" Robert said.

"Aye," Patrick and Freddie answered in unison, their voices heavily tinged with husky arousal.

"All right now." Robert laughed and delivered the first playful slap to her bottom.

"Ooh," Celia breathed in response. The next little smack landed on her other butt cheek, followed by a third and on and on in succession until her bottom tingled and her entire sex throbbed and ached, wanting only to be filled and brought to release. Her body grew so languid that she couldn't support her weight on her hands and sunk onto the mattress in the middle of them.

Patrick laughed. "Think she's had enough, lads?"

"She never has enough," Freddie said.

"Let's give her more then," Robert added. He slid down onto his back and tugged her gently up. "Come, Ceil, climb on me. Freddie and Patrick will take care of the rest."

Eagerly, Celia obeyed, coming to life and feeling her way around so that she could straddle Robert's groin. She was so wet and open from her spanking that she slid down easily on to his erection.

Robert held her hips, stroking them in smooth circles. "Do ye want to do what we have planned fer ye, Ceil?"

She nodded vigorously. "Aye, very much so."

"You know we'd never do anything to hurt ye?"

"I do know that."

Robert chuckled and squeezed the swells of her hips. "Right then. Lean forward and give Patrick room back there.

Celia did as he told her and felt Patrick move behind her. Reaching to her face, he brushed his fingertips across her lips. "Give me some spit, Ceil."

She murmured and took his fingers into her mouth, suckling them eagerly.

"That's good," Patrick whispered, pulling his fingers from her mouth and smoothing the moisture over her bottom hole.

He pushed a finger in gently and moved it around. She let out a sharp breath of pleasure as the sensation pushed Robert's erection more tightly inside her. "How is that, Ceil?"

"Very good."

"Okay."

Robert played with her breasts while Patrick pushed the head of his cock into her arse, wetting his hand with more spit and slathering it on his cock to make him slippery. Inch by delightful inch, he slid in carefully until he was completely inside her.

Celia moaned as both men filled her. Instinctively, she began to rock back and forth, causing both of them to slide in and out. Her hands sank into the mattress on either side of Robert's chest as she found a gentle rhythm. All thoughts melted away and her heart raced as she succumbed completely to being filled.

A gentle hand cupped her chin, turning her head. Freddie had moved up and now knelt close to her face, the head of his hard cock nudging her lips. He slid his thumb across her lips as they parted, inviting the swollen taut head between them.

Freddie tasted delicious, the silky skin of his penis gliding against her tongue. She heard him groan as he slid more deeply into her mouth, having her take him in as much as she could. His movements against her mouth fell into a rhythm with her body.

Every part of her that could be was now filled with a man. A moan erupted deep in her throat, vibrating softly around Freddie's shaft. His fingers were laced in her hair, his hands following her head, only pushing himself into her mouth as much as she could take him.

"Oh my God," she heard Patrick mutter. He began to thrust more rapidly inside her, his hands anchored on her hips. "It's so tight in there." His movements pushed Robert's cock tightly against her clitoris and a shattering of lights exploded behind the darkness of her blindfold as the tiny muscle contracted.

After several moments, she felt his body jerk behind her. His hands tightened on her hips and she felt his cock pulsing warm seed inside her. He slipped out and sat back, breathing heavily.

Celia sat up on Robert now, grinding against him, still completely weakened from the incredible experience. She leaned over slightly, squeezing her muscles around his shaft.

Robert groaned, his hands lightly gripping her waist. "That's it, Ceil," he rasped out, "That's me girl." He released a tight suction of breath and Celia felt his climax inside her, his hot seed gushing, filling her. He held her in place on top of him, his chest rising and falling heavily. "Slow down, Ceil," he breathed. "Give Freddie your complete attention."

Celia was happy to obey. She loved the feel of Freddie's hardness against her tongue. The smooth skin tasted delicious and his musky scent filled her. She cupped his balls in one hand while she suckled him, running her tongue up and down his length and over the swollen head.

Freddie groaned and suddenly pulled out of her mouth. Warm milky seed shot out and landed on her chin and chest. "Thank you, Ceil," he murmured between heavy breaths.

She laughed softly, as joy welled up inside of her. Her mind and body were completely saturated and drunk from the men she loved and her heart warmed with contentment and joy.

She felt a hand at her head, lifting off the blindfold. She blinked several times, allowing her eyes to adjust to the light, blurry as they were from the blindfold.

Freddie reached for a handkerchief and loving wiped her face.

Robert tugged her down to lie on her back. He kissed her lips. "How was that for you, Ceil?" he asked, caressing her hair back, off her face.

Celia heaved a deep sigh of satisfaction. "That was the most incredible experience of my entire life," she breathed. "I love you all so much. Thank you."

"Nothing to thank us for," Robert said gently. He lay down with his head on her stomach while Freddie and

Patrick also lay down on either side of her, the way they had for so many years. Only this time, all four of them were naked.

Celia closed her eyes, her fingertips toying lovingly with Robert's soft dark hair. She smiled to herself and reveled in being completely surrounded by warm masculine strength, grateful for having been given another chance.

Love was her freedom, and she felt herself falling, joyfully falling into completeness.

~ * ~

THE SATISFACTION OF
CELIA FLYNN

Ballykilmarrick, Ireland
March, 1918

"I propose a toast." Robert held up his wineglass and stood. The ruby liquid shone from the hearth fire behind him. "To our great fortune."

Celia held up her glass in agreement, as did Freddie and Patrick. The sting of happy tears rushed to her eyes. Good fortune, indeed.

She watched Robert's gaze move from one of them to the next. His usual mischievous grin tugged at his lips and his dimples creased the planes of his cheeks. "We have much to be grateful for this night," he went on. His dark eyes shone and the firelight glinted off the rich brown color of his short hair.

"We three lads returned from war alive and basically whole. Celia was here, ready for us, wanting us to love her again." He inclined his head toward the nearby cradle, which sat close enough to the fire for warmth, yet far enough for safety from sparks. "And there's a healthy, ruddy-cheeked babe in that cradle, one year old today, Tommy is, a product of my and Ceil's love." A sparkle came into his eye and he shot a look at Patrick and Freddie. "God willing, there'll be more of those by you two lads down the road."

"Here, here," Patrick and Freddie answered in unison.

Celia laughed softly. Her cheeks tingled pleasantly, both from Robert's comment and from the bit of wine she'd had during their celebration dinner.

Robert's grin widened. "And," he continued, a suggestive note in his voice, "Our mother-in-law, the lovely Margaret Flynn, is in Dublin until tomorrow evening."

"Here, here," Patrick and Freddie piped in again, their voices a male chorus that made the tingle in Celia's cheeks spread lower, flush through her breasts and down, into her sex.

Celia knew precisely what Robert meant.

Robert raised his glass higher. "So tonight, we drink to good fortune in all its faces. Not that we don't appreciate Margaret and how hard she's worked to accept all three of us loving her daughter at once, but…" He shot a devilish grin at Celia. "On a night like this when we have the house all to ourselves, we can descend upon our lass, all three of us, rather than hold to the compromise we have made for Margaret's comfort."

A delightful shudder of warmth passed through Celia's entire body. The lads' concession to Celia's mother had been that each man would each take his turn in Celia's bed. One man, one night at a time.

Robert leaned in and clinked his glass against all the others. The four of them sipped their wine and set the glasses down. Celia's head swam now, not from the drink but from the prospect of loving all three of her lads at once. It had been a long time since the last and no doubt, Robert would have something fun planned to heighten their pleasure.

"Celia." Robert was gazing at her. Desire darkened his face. "I suggest we leave the dishes for the morrow and not put off our celebration a moment longer."

His look and words sent a frisson of lust through her sex. She nodded. "Aye. I agree."

Robert grinned. "I thought ye might. And so, I have our special place all prepared. Lady and gentlemen, follow me." He pulled Celia's chair out for her. When she rose to her feet, he took her hand and pressed his lips into her palm. His eyes simmered into hers with promise.

Celia's body tingled wildly at Robert's mere touch. She caught her breath. Robert always had the most delightful and pleasurable activities planned for her, even when it was just the two of them.

He released her hand. "The lads and I guarantee your satisfaction this night, Ceil." He winked and turned, starting for the door. He still limped from the shrapnel he'd taken in the hip, but he no longer needed his cane to walk.

Anxious to begin their interlude, Celia picked up Patrick's hand and placed it on her shoulder to guide him. Patrick had been blinded by mustard gas in the trenches, but even though his green eyes were sightless, he swore he could see her face when he looked at her.

Together, they trailed into the back parlour.

With a flourish, Freddie opened the door for her. Celia stepped in, Patrick close behind her. As soon as she saw the room, she stopped and stared. Her heart thumped. Now she understood why Robert had spent so much time in the parlour that afternoon with the door closed, forbidding her to enter. "Robert!" she breathed.

Gauzy white lengths of cloth hung from the ceiling, draping down create an intimate space in the center of the small room. Boughs of Scots fir rested on the window seats, tabletops and mantel, giving the room the appearance of a small forest glade. The scent of pine permeated the air and burned in the hearth, which crackled pleasantly and made the room cozy.

Robert had cleared the center of the rug and set down a luxurious-looking pile of blankets and cushions. "I hope you'll be comfortable here, Ceil," he said as he set the cradle down in a warm, safe corner of the room.

Celia's heartbeat sped up and tears rushed to her eyes. She was most definitely the luckiest lass in all the world. "Robert, it's splendid!" Her voice came out in a breathy rush. "I can't believe you went to all this trouble. Thank you."

Robert came up beside her and kissed her cheek. "I only want the best for our lass," he said softly. He picked up her hand and tugged gently. "Now, come this way, to the center of the glen." He grinned and led Celia to the middle of the clearing.

Celia slipped off her shoes and let her stockinged feet sink into the bedding. Immediately she found herself surrounded by Robert, Freddie and Patrick. Their closeness sent a thrill through her. It had been a very long time since the three of them had all been this close together. She swallowed hard as her heartbeat sped up.

"Now, lassie," Robert said, mischief in his tone, "The last *I* looked, wood faeries weren't wearing skirts and blouses." He reached up and undid the top button of Celia's blouse.

Celia took a deep breath. Robert's fingers brushed the skin of her throat. He undid several more buttons and Celia felt the warm air touch her skin above the lace edging of her camisole.

"Ahh, so beautiful," Robert murmured. "Look lads, skin like fresh cream." He brushed the fingertips of one hand across the top of her chest. His touch sent delightful shivers through her and her nipples tingled.

"Aye," Patrick said softly. "The softest thing in the whole world." He ran the pads of his fingers down the side of Celia's neck. "And her neck is so graceful, like a swan." He leaned in and pressed his lips to the side of her neck.

She sighed and tiled her head.

Patrick responded by pressing in closer. He parted his lips and Celia felt the moist warmth of his tongue brush her sensitive skin.

She sighed and parted her lips. Suddenly, Robert kissed her, claimed her mouth in that special way he had. Celia always knew Robert's gentle yet commanding way with her. Knew it blindfolded...

Robert swiped his tongue across hers, teased and coaxed Celia to hot arousal. Freddie picked up her hand and suckled on her fingers. One by one, he licked the exquisitely sensitive pads of Celia's fingers. The wet heat of his tongue weakened her, made her moan.

Celia's eyelids shuttered. Her body felt languid, and her sex pulsed with gathering need. Her three lads always left her weak and breathless, unable to do anything except let them take possession of her. Hands moved all over her, over her breasts, her bottom, her back and stomach. Fingers here and there finished undoing the buttons of her blouse and the fastenings of her skirt. The clothing dropped to the floor around her feet, leaving her in only her camisole, drawers, garters and stockings.

Robert lifted his lips from hers. His dark eyes simmered more than ever and his full lips looked as swollen and moist from kissing as Celia's felt. He grinned. "Now one of the best parts," he murmured and pulled the string at the top of her camisole.

The lacy material fell open, revealing the tops of Celia's breasts.

"Celia," Robert breathed, "Ye are the prettiest thing." His eyelids lowered in a sensual way and he took her mouth again.

The other lads continued to caress her. Patrick stole under the camisole with both hands and cupped her breasts. Celia moaned softly and sagged back against him. His lips remained pressed tenderly on the side of her neck and he feathered the tip of his tongue on her skin while he squeezed her breasts and pinched her nipples, teased them lovingly into taut peaks.

Freddie knelt before her. He loved her thighs very much and always told her so. But Celia knew that anyway because whenever they were together, he spent much time kissing and stroking them as he did now. With teasing fingertips he caressed her inner thighs and rained soft kisses on the supple skin there.

He pulled the string of her drawers and let them fall around her feet with the rest of her clothes. Her bare sex was a mere few inches away from his face now.

"Celia," she heard him whisper in a throaty voice. His hot breath passed over the front of her moist core. He slid his fingertips up one of her thighs and the grazed them down the length of her slit.

Celia threw her head back. She was absorbed, mind, body and soul in the touches and kisses of her three lads. Thank goodness Patrick stood behind her, supporting her sagging weight because she could barely stand up now from the erotic bliss invading her body.

Back and forth, Freddie caressed the moist crevice of Celia's sex. He ventured a bit deeper inside with each gentle swipe until he brushed over the hard swollen nub at the center.

Celia cried out softly, the sound muffled by Robert's deep kiss. Robert swiped his tongue across hers and then pulled away.

"Come, lads," he said.

Obediently, Freddie and Patrick ceased touching and kissing her. Celia's eyes flew open and she nearly went dizzy from the sudden cold absence of hands and mouths on her body. Her gaze fell on Robert who, of course, was grinning like the devil himself.

He held out a hand. "Freddie, your tie, please, lad."

"Aye." Freddie quickly undid the knot in his tie and worked it open.

Celia's heart thumped and a frisson of heat passed through her.

"Patrick," Robert said, "Remove Celia's cammy."

"Aye." Patrick was still behind Celia, the heat of his body close to hers. Gently, he felt for the hem of her camisole and lifted it. His fingertips grazed her skin deliciously as he slid the flimsy material up, past her breasts.

Celia lifted her arms for him and let him pull the article all the way off. Patrick dropped it aside. "May I touch her again, Robert?" he breathed.

Robert chuckled. "Soon, mate."

"Here's my tie."

"Thanks, mate." Robert took the tie from him and grinned at Celia. "Hold out your hands, lassie."

Another ripple of erotic heat passed through Celia's body. She obeyed and Robert gently bound her wrists.

"Remember that night back in the inn in Edinburgh, when we fetched Freddie from the hospital?" Robert said in a husky voice.

Celia nearly went breathless. "Aye."

Robert chuckled. "I would have thought so. Well, tonight, we're going to play the same game of *Guess Who?* only with a twist." He reached out and brushed his fingertips across Celia's cheek, trailed them down the side of her neck and pulled away. "Last time, Ceil, you had to guess by touch which lad was which. Tonight, you will try and guess who is touching you…" He traced the swell of her right breast with gentle fingertips.

Celia caught her breath.

"Tasting you," he went on. As he'd done earlier, he picked up her hand and held it to his lips for a brief kiss. "All while blindfolded and bound." He kissed her hand again, feathered the tip of his tongue on the sensitive inside of her wrist. "How does that sound, lass?"

Celia breathed heavily. Whispers of tingling heat spiraled through her body and she felt how wet and open her sex already was. "That sounds wonderful."

Robert squeezed her hand. "Very well then. Lie down here and we'll prepare you for the game." He helped her to lie down on the cushions on her back. Freddie and Patrick helped stuff the pillows underneath her so that her breasts and her lower body were raised. "Are you comfortable, Ceil?" Robert asked when they'd finished.

She nodded. "Aye. Very." Her voice came out breathless and every inch of her body was weak with desire.

"Excellent. Now, you have a choice. Before the blindfold goes on, do you wish to watch us undress?"

"Oh, aye." The mere suggestion sent another jolt of heat through her sex. She loved watching the lads undress, loved seeing them uncover their beautiful masculine bodies bit by bit.

"Very well. Get on with it then, lads. Give our lady what she wants." Robert's grin widened as his hands went to his tie, which he loosened slowly, as if to tease Celia.

Celia looked at Freddie. He'd already unbuttoned his shirt. The firelight glinted off his short golden hair and pale skin. A surge of heat passed through her middle. Freddie had a sleekly sculpted body, slim yet hard. His muscles flexed as he lifted off his undershirt, revealing the sprinkling of dark golden hair on his chest and tawny nipples.

Celia swallowed hard and looked at Patrick. He too, had stripped off his shirt and undershirt and was undoing his trousers. Patrick's build was between Freddie's and Robert's in musculature. Patrick was athletic and still loved to play football even though he couldn't see. His love of movement was reflected in the rounded hardness of his shoulders and chest. He turned slightly to take off his pants and gave Celia a perfect view of his hard buttocks flexing against the tight material of his drawers.

A lustful shiver tore through her whole body. The sound and movement of clothing coming undone and falling to the floor was all around her.

She looked at Robert. His heavy lidded gaze was on her. He'd just finished unbuttoning his shirt and slipped it off. Celia nearly moaned at the sight of Robert's torso, at the bulge of his farmer's physique under the form-fitting undershirt he wore. The dark, silky hairs of his chest peeped over the top and Celia licked her lips. He unbuckled his trousers as slowly as he'd worked off his tie. Mischief glinted in his dark eyes and Celia remained captured, watching him undress until his whole muscular body was naked, thick erection and all.

As a matter of fact, all three of them no longer wore a stitch…

Robert picked up a scarf and knelt by Celia's head. "And now, for the blindfold…" He covered her eyes and tied the scarf firmly but gently. That done, he took her bound wrists and lifted her arms above her head. "Now, we can begin. Remember, lads, the only rule of this game is that no one gets Celia off." He chuckled. "That is, until the last bit when all three of us get her off at once. *If* she wins the game."

Celia caught her breath. Oh, God, she was already in heaven and they'd barely touched her.

"Ready, Ceil?" Robert said.

She nodded. "Aye."

"Very good. Round one begins. I'll let you know when to give your answers."

Silence fell over the room, the only sound being the crackle of the fire. Celia's body tingled in anticipation.

The heat of a male body filled the space around her and she felt someone kneel between her spread legs and hover over her. He leaned into her, breath warm on her face and lowered his lips to hers.

Celia sighed. She immediately recognized Robert's earthy musky scent. From the moment their lips touched, she knew for sure it was him. He took her mouth in that commanding yet gentle way of his, slipped his tongue past the seam of her lips and tasted her with strong passion. The kiss didn't last long, for he pulled away and rained a trail of kisses down her neck and chest.

Strong, tender hands palmed her breasts, drew them upward together. Robert's touch. No doubt in her mind, and body.

She sighed again, her whole body warm and melty under his possession. He licked and suckled her nipples, squeezed her breasts together before he released them and moved lower. The same gentle yet commanding touch landed on both thighs and slid upward. He slipped his thumbs between the soft folds of her sex and spread her open.

Celia's breath caught. Robert swiped his tongue over her clit, teased it with small flickers. He pushed one finger inside her at the same time and made her cry out softly from the invasion of pleasure.

That was definitely Robert.

Then he was gone.

The second man replaced him between her spread thighs and leaned over her prone body. His yummy scent of aftershave and soap gave him away immediately.

Celia murmured happily and strained lightly against her bonds, stretched her body upward in anticipation of the next touch.

First his kiss. Mmm, just as she'd known -- Patrick. She could never mistake the worshipful, sweet way he kissed her. First he brushed his lips across hers, back and forth several times as if begging her to open. When she did, he dipped his tongue in and swirled it sensuously around, so obviously trying to please her. Celia loved kissing Patrick and moved her tongue against his in that sweet dance they had.

He groaned softly. He tried to suppress it, by the sound, and pulled his lips from hers. He slid his hands to her breasts, caressed the soft swells with his heated passion. Sex was still rather new to him -- Celia having been his first and only lass. Celia felt the coiled up energy in his hands. How gentle he was. His touch radiated tentative sweetness and made her feel so worshiped and beautiful. He slid his hands to her back, cradling her and licked her nipples, suckled them so lightly at first then with increasing pressure.

Celia arched upward, lost in the pleasure. She moaned softy as Patrick lifted away from her breasts and moved his feast to her sex.

His large hands cupped her buttocks, gently lifted her, and he pressed his mouth to her inner sex. He closed his lips and tongue over the hard, sensitive nub and suckled gently, as if he were drinking her essence.

Aye, this was Patrick and no other.

As Robert had done before him, Patrick pleasured her only long enough to leave her panting, her back arched in a plea for more, and then he, too, was gone, replaced by her third delicious lad.

Freddie, unmistakable by his clean scent of maleness and, oddly, paper, lowered his slimmer form between her legs. His breathing was light and quick and Celia sensed his ever-present concern to pleasure her. Freddie made love to her as he lived, a mathematician at heart and by trade. He kissed her slowly and precisely, making sure he didn't miss a spot of her lips and tongue.

He kissed a soft, intent trail over her jaw and down her neck, a nearly perfect straight line to the valley between her small breasts. He rounded each taut nipple with his tongue, traced the exact shape of the dusky puckered skin and dark red tip before continuing his perfect line down the center of her stomach to her sex.

Celia giggled softly, both from delight and from the light ticklish feeling of Freddie's perfect kisses. His perfectionism delighted her and also inspired her compassion. He'd come a long way in less than two years of having suffered shell shock from the war.

Freddie spread Celia's sex open with gentle fingers and kissed the center. He swiveled his tongue around her aching clit and up and down the opening of her sex.

Celia cried out softly. Freddie's precise loving brought her body brought to a pitch of arousal.

Her three lads were torturing her, pure and simple. Aye, it was the most delightful torment, but her body needed release now, so desperately.

Freddie pulled away and then he was gone.

She heard Robert chuckle. "Well, Ceil, who was who?"

"Robert, Patrick, Freddie," she breathed. Her body coursed with need, her mind dizzy.

"Very good, lass. Now for the second round. Get that right and you'll have your satisfaction."

Celia felt more than one pair of hands slide under her and lift her. Gently, her lads turned her over until she was on her knees, supporting her front with her elbows. Someone stuffed cushions under her hips and belly, giving her extra support.

"Ready for the next round?" Robert said. Delightful mischief laced his tone.

"Aye," Celia said, nearly breathless.

A moment passed and one of her lads knelt behind her. His male warmth pressed close and large gentle hands closed on her hips. Celia knew Patrick's touch immediately. He nudged her opening with the head of his cock in the way he always did, as if asking for her permission to take her.

She pushed back against him. Her sex was so slick and open he slid right in. Patrick's cock fit her just right and his gentle yet passionate thrusts reminded her always of their first time. He panted, moaned softly, as he'd done before. His cock reached deep inside her, touched all the delicious paces that made her cry out with delight each time. When his cock twitched inside her, she knew he was about to come. She squeezed her lower muscles around him and heard him groan in response. Another squeeze and he came, filled her with his warm seed.

He collapsed over her back, caressed her hips for several moments, then slipped out.

Her next lad took Patrick's place. He closed his hands on her hips.

Robert. Celia recognized his firm, tender touch. Her body always relaxed in his hold because he made her feel so safe, so held.

She felt him guide the head of his cock to her opening. He slipped in and gently pushed.

Aye, there was no mistaking that thick meaty part of him that filled her.

He thrust gently but firmly, an even rhythm that touched her deep inside. She wanted to come so badly and lifted her hips, but even though he was large, Robert's cock didn't hit the spot that would give her release. Each time their bodies met a jolt of pleasure shivered through her sex.

The torture built. Celia cried out each time, completely, utterly lost in this whole enchanting night.

Robert moved faster and faster, rubbed her soft insides with his thick cock until he, too, came. His hands tightened on her hips and he held her to him until he'd emptied his climax.

He slipped out moments later, left her body wanting and unfulfilled.

Freddie replaced him only moments later. His erection was slimmer than Patrick's and Robert's, but no less amazing, no less filling as he thrust inside her. Of course, he followed an even, precise rhythm, his breath matching the tempo of his movements. He held her hips gently, caressed them, and made certain to stroke her thighs too. His attention to her thighs was what would have given him away if Celia hadn't already known so well the feeling of his cock inside her.

All too soon, Freddie climaxed. All three lads had come sooner than usual, probably wound up as they were by the intense eroticism of their activity. Celia, however, hadn't even come once and her body ached so much she was at the point of begging for release.

"All right, Ceil. Who was who?" Robert said in his wicked tone.

"Patrick, you, Freddie."

All three lads laughed. "Aye, that's our lass," Patrick said.

Someone pulled her blindfold off and someone else unbound her wrists. Celia blinked and focused on the three handsome faces hovering above her, at the contrast of their hair, Robert's dark, dark brown, Patrick's chestnut and

Freddie's golden tone. She smiled at them, still panting. "Well, now, please?"

They grinned down at her and leaned forward. Hands all over Celia turned her onto her back and arranged the cushions as before. In the next moment, Robert leaned down and claimed her mouth. His skin was hot and damp and his tongue swirled hungrily against hers.

Celia sighed and surrendered to the kiss. In no time, Patrick leaned over her breasts and licked and suckled her nipples the way he'd done before, one hand caressing her stomach at the same time.

On instinct, Celia wound her fingers into his hair and moaned into Robert's mouth.

Then Freddie knelt by her sex. He kissed the inside of one thigh and caressed the other with gentle fingertips. His kissed moved upward, dangerously close...

Celia felt the hot moist press of his tongue on her clit.

Oh! She closed her eyes as pleasure tingled in every inch. All three men were kissing, suckling and caressing her at once and her whole existence distilled to these sensations.

Freddie spread her thighs wider apart and slipped two fingers in her passage while he licked her clit in wild circles.

In seconds, Celia burst. Her orgasm plowed through her sex in wave after wave. Her lads never stopped their licks and caresses until her body went limp and sagged underneath their mouths and hands.

Robert gave her one last peck on the lips and settled down beside her, one hand caressing her cheek. Patrick snuggled against her, his arm draped over her middle while Freddie used one of her thighs as a pillow.

"Well, Ceil, how was that?" Robert asked softly. "Special, I hope, for you as it was for us."

Celia smiled and covered his hand with hers. She sighed a deep breath and felt deliciously cocooned by the heat emanating off the masculine bodies surrounding her. "Ahhh," she said, hearing the utter contentment in her voice, "when I float back down from Heaven, I'll tell you."

THE END

Sedonia Guillone

Sedonia Guillone lives on the water in Florida in winter and on the rocky coast of Maine in summers with a Renaissance man who paints, writes poetry and tells her she's the sweetest nymph he's ever met. When she's not writing erotic romance, she loves watching spaghetti westerns, cuddling, and eating chocolate.

Visit Sedonia on the Web at www.sedoniaguillone.com.

ANTHOLOGIES & SINGLE AUTHOR OMNIBUS TITLES
available in print from Loose Id®

HARD CANDY
Angela Knight, Morgan Hawke and Sheri Gilmore

HOWL
Jet Mykles, Raine Weaver, and Jeigh Lynn

RATED: X-MAS
Rachel Bo, Barbara Karmazin and Jet Mykles

THE BITE BEFORE CHRISTMAS
Laura Baumbach, Sedonia Guillone and Kit Tunstall

THE SYNDICATE
Jules Jones & Alex Woolgrave

ALPHA
Treva Harte

STRENGTH IN NUMBERS
Rachel Bo

THE PRENDARIAN CHRONICLES
Doreen DeSalvo